RICHARD SEIDMAN

CATALYST GROUP  ASHLAND, OREGON

Summary:
Louis LaSurie aspires to be the first mouse in the world to play for France in the World Cup Soccer tournament.

Print Edition: ISBN: 978-0-9898553-0-3
EPUB Edition: ISBN: 978-0-9898553-1-0

Illustrations: Ursula Andrejczuk
Book Design: Chris Molé Design

In recognition of the paper used to create and market this book, the author will contribute a percentage of the profits to Friends of Trees, the nonprofit tree-planting group he founded in Portland, Oregon, USA. He will also contribute to organizations that support youth soccer in the US and around the world.

World Cup Mouse

CHAPTER 1

Danger in the Library

A ROCK SHATTERED ON THE SIDEWALK three inches in front of Louie LaSurie.

"Get out of here!" a man shouted. "Next time I won't miss." He clapped his hands. "Shoo!"

Louie froze in place, whiskers trembling and eyes opened wide. He had been daydreaming about playing soccer as he trotted down the sidewalk toward the Marseille Public Library. He should have been paying better attention.

Animals and humans could speak with each other, of course. But Louie's mother said it was safer not to. "Humans are too unpredictable," she warned. "A lot of them are nice enough, but some of them hate mice."

This man was obviously one of the haters. But Louie was mad now. He forgot about his mother's advice. "Why should I get out of here?"

The man sneered. "Why? Because you're vermin.

You're just a mouse. You're nothing."

Louie clenched his paws. "I'm not nothing! I'm *somebody*!"

The man snorted and stomped away.

"I'm somebody!" Louie yelled again. "And you're a dope," he added under his breath.

His face hot with anger, Louie sprinted the rest of the way to the library. *In fact*, Louie thought, *I'm not just any somebody. I'm somebody who's going to be the first mouse soccer player in the history of the world!*

Louie squeezed under the door. The library was closed this late at night. He shook off the raindrops clinging to his beret. He stood still for a moment and breathed in the delightful smell of books. Then he shot across the cool marble floor of the lobby to the magazine room. He shimmied up the leg of a reading table in the sports section.

Louie was in luck. An article about the 1982 World Cup tournament was lying open on top of the table. With the newspaper spread out under him, Louie scampered back and forth across the page as he read each line of text.

What a team France had back then! What great players. Platini. Giresse. Tigana. He read how France lost to Germany in a penalty kick shootout in the semifinals. Louie groaned.

Jingle-clink. What was that? It sounded like jangling keys. Louie lifted his head.

A man carrying a mop and a bucket of water sprang into the reading room.The janitor!

The man yelled, "*Et voilà*! Now I've got you, you scoundrel."

Louie gasped. He was too shocked to run away. "I was only reading," he said.

The man wore a nametag over his left breast that read, *Gaston Trudeau*. "I don't care," Gaston said. "I don't allow mice in my library."

Louie was about to say, "It's not *your* library," but he had no time because the janitor ran straight at him with the mop raised over his head.

Louie jumped off the table all the way to the floor. The impact knocked the wind out of him.

The janitor bounded toward him.

Gasping for breath, Louie dodged between the man's legs.

The janitor turned around fast. The mop came smashing down in an explosion of dust right next to Louie's head. It sounded like a million firecrackers.

Louie saw stars. He didn't know where he was any more. He ran straight up the inside of the janitor's pant leg. The hairs on the man's leg made Louie sneeze.

Gaston did a frantic dance and Louie tumbled back to the floor.

The man lifted his foot.

Louie saw the huge boot flying right at him. He rolled to his right.

The boot came crashing down a half inch from Louie's chest.

Louie scrambled under a table. His heart was pounding like mad.

The janitor, on hands and knees, followed him, poking at him with the mop handle.

"Please, calm down," Louie panted.

"I will *not* calm down!" Gaston yelled. He made a quick thrust with his mop and Louie felt a flash of pain as the mop handle slammed onto his tail, pinning him to the wall.

He was trapped!

CHAPTER 2

The Most Fun Any Mouse Could Have

LOUIE WIGGLED AND SHOOK, but he couldn't get loose. His whole body trembled and his tail felt like it was on fire. He bit one of his whiskers to keep from crying. The story of how he had gotten into this mess flashed through his brain.

Two years earlier, when he was still a little mouse, Louie had sneaked up to the baker's apartment above his family's nest to see if the baker might be watching television. The TV was blaring. Excellent! He scooted to a viewing spot under an old, maroon sofa.

Louie wasn't sure where the baker stood on the issue of talking with animals, so he thought it was safer to stay out of sight.

He settled into his hiding place and looked at the TV screen. Men were chasing a white ball across a green, grassy field, kicking it and occasionally hitting

it with their heads. Louie's jaw dropped. It was the most magnificent thing he had ever seen. His whole body tingled. His heart soared along with the ball as it flew through the air. For a few moments, everything around him dropped away. All that was left was beauty.

Following the TV commentator's words, Louie soon understood the purpose of the game. When one of the players kicked the ball into the goal, Louie laughed out loud. He ran around beneath the sofa with his paws up in the air.

Sometimes the baker's gigantic flour-covered shoes blocked Louie's view, so he'd have to scoot over to see the screen. When the baker shifted position, the sofa creaked loudly overhead. It was dusty under there, and noisy, but Louie didn't mind. He had found what he loved.

Simply watching the soccer game was fantastic, but to play it...oh, that would be the most fun he could ever have.

The next day at recess, he tracked down his best friend. "François," Louie announced, "I'm going to become a soccer player."

François DuBois was a roly-poly, good-natured mouse. He stared at Louie through his glasses. "What?"

"You know, kicking the ball and all that."

"I've heard of soccer," François said. "I just never heard of mice playing it."

"I'll be the first."

François smiled. "Great. If anyone can do it, you can."

"First," Louie said, "I need to get in shape and practice. And second, I have to study the game."

That's exactly what Louie had done these past two years. He perfected kicking and dribbling his soccer ball, a dried pea borrowed from his mother's kitchen. He played soccer every day with François. Many times he tried to interest his brothers and sisters in the game, but they were all older than Louie and viewed his enthusiasm as a childish fantasy and were never interested.

"Sorry, Louie, I'm too busy," said his oldest brother, Stuart.

"Me too," said Bianca, the next oldest.

"Same with me," said Elizabeth.

And so on for Martin, Bernard, and Norman.

It was the same at school. Louie put up posters and talked to his friends and tried to arrange soccer games at recess or after school, but the other mice only laughed at him.

Louie was not deterred. He watched games at the baker's and read everything he could find about the sport. He studied soccer history and strategy and coaching methods. His studies were what had brought him to the library on this damp night. (The mouse library in his neighborhood didn't have any materials on soccer.) And that's what had gotten him trapped and might now cost him his life.

Louie looked down the long mop handle toward the janitor's smug smile.

"I knew it was only a matter of time before I caught you," the man gloated. "Who do you think you are, anyway, coming in here like this?"

"I should be allowed to use the library like any other citizen of Marseille," Louie squeaked. It was difficult to talk with the mop pressing hard on his tail and terror tightening his throat.

"A citizen of Marseille?" The janitor laughed. "You're just a mouse. You're nothing. You're nobody."

There was that phrase again. "I'm not nobody!" Louie yelled. He tightened his muscles. He wriggled madly and, with a great shout like a karate guy, "Hi-ya!", flung himself free.

Gaston swore as Louie scooted under a bookshelf.

Louie hid there, panting. He moved his tail to see if it still worked. It ached, but at least it didn't seem broken.

After a long time, Louie watched the man's feet walk away. "It's not fair!" Louie shouted, his paws clenched into fists.

"Life isn't fair, mousie," Gaston muttered from across the room. "Get used to it."

Louie scurried to the front door, squeezed under it, and ran all the way home through the rain-soaked streets. The janitor's words, like those of that other man on the street, stung more than his sore tail. "Just a mouse." "Nothing." "Nobody."

He'd show that mean janitor. He'd show everyone. He was not a nothing. He'd play real soccer or he'd die trying!

CHAPTER 3

“Where there’s a mouse, there’s a way!”

LOUIE SNEAKED BACK INTO HIS NEST and found his bed, a dented tart pan lined with an old sock. Snores and murmurs told him the rest of his family was still asleep. Gradually, his breathing calmed down. As the aroma of baking croissants drifted down the stairs from the bakery and mingled with the comforting smell of the sock, he too fell asleep. He dreamed.

He’s a member of the French World Cup soccer team, the only mouse on the field. Louie waves his paw to show that he’s open.

The captain of the French team, Abidad Rouzon, passes the ball to him.

Louie kicks it hard, feeling the thump of the ball on his right rear paw. He watches the ball sail inches beyond the leaping goalie’s outstretched fingers. Goaaalll!

Louie slides on his knees along the grass with his arms

raised in celebration. Yes!

All the French players mob him, tousling his head and slapping his back, gently, with their index or pinkie fingers.

The crowd chants, "Lou-ie! Lou-ie! Lou-ie!"

"Louie! Louie! Louie!" His father was shaking him. "Wake up. You'll be late for school."

Louie sat up and blinked. Staring at his tattered sock bed, he sighed and sank back down. How could he ever play for France? He was only two and a half inches tall standing on his tiptoes. He was the shortest mouse in his class. Compared to humans, he was really, *really* short.

Louie pulled on his pants and put his hind paws into his sneakers. Many great players were short. Messi, Xavi, George Best, Maradona, Pelé. He had learned about all of them in the course of his studies.

Of course, he admitted as he yanked his purple turtleneck over his head, none of them was a mouse. He punched his paw in the air and cried, "There's always a first to everything! Where there's a mouse, there's a way!"

"That's not necessarily true, Louie," his father said from the hall. He walked back into the bedroom. "Just because you want something doesn't mean you can get it." His father ruffled Louie's head fur. "And how could you ever play with humans anyway? You're just a mouse."

Louie jerked away from his father's touch. There

was that saying again. *Just a mouse*. "I'd play in a mouse league, Papa, or even some other kind of animal league, but there aren't any. It's play with humans, or don't play at all. And if I'm going to play with humans, why not play with the best?"

Louie's mother entered the room.

"Play with the best?" Louie's father said. "It's ridiculous! Grandiose." His plump mouse belly shook with laughter. "I'm sorry to laugh, Louie, but the humans won't even see you."

"*Mon Dieu*," Louie's mother rubbed her front paws together. "Isn't soccer awfully dangerous? I mean, you might get squished."

Louie put his paws on his hips. "I will be the first mouse to play in the World Cup or I will get squished in the attempt! Where there's a mouse, there's a way!"

Louie's mother sighed. His father's whiskers twitched.

Louie heard them talking as they walked down the hallway. "Don't worry, my dear," his father said. "I'm sure this is merely a phase that will pass."

"It's not 'merely a phase'!" Louie shouted. It might be ridiculous, but it was not a phase. He loved soccer and he always would.

Louie was determined to prove them wrong. He did even more conditioning drills to increase his fitness: pushups, sit-ups, jumping jacks, and darting up and down the inside of walls.

He kicked his dried-pea ball everywhere around the house and in the alley.

He even taught himself sewing and shoemaking in order to make a soccer jersey, shin guards, soccer shorts and cleats. None of these items were available in Mousie's or WalMouse, the two stores where the family did their shopping. Many a night found Louie bent over one of his projects, needle and thread in paw, while his family joked and laughed in the next room.

"Ouch!" Louie cried one night when he pricked himself with the needle. He threw his project down to the floor in frustration. The sounds of his family's laughter in the next room made the pain in his paw worse. "I'm missing out on all the fun," he grumbled. But then Louie took a deep breath, squared his shoulders and dusted off the half-finished jersey. "No," he told himself. "A mouse like me does not give up."

Louie and François worked hard one weekend and built a staircase out of fifty-two bottle caps staggered and stuck together with old chewing gum.

"On your mark, get set—go!" François shouted. Louie sprinted up and then jogged down the bottle cap stairway. Louie ran this course over and over until his legs quavered.

All the time, though, doubts and fears whispered inside Louie's own head. That he was just a mouse, a nobody, a nothing. And his hope to play soccer was absurd.

It couldn't be true, could it?

CHAPTER 4

Old Giresse

LOUIE WALKED TO SCHOOL one morning a week after the library incident.

"Psst. Hey, Shortie."

Louie looked around. Who was that?

"Over here." A mouse was waving to him from behind a garbage can.

Louie approached cautiously.

He was an elderly mouse, dressed in tatters. His fur was grayish-white and his brown eyes were bleary with age. "Don't let them crush your dreams, Shortie." The old mouse's voice was hoarse and weak.

"How do you know about my dreams?"

"Been watching you and Old DuBois's great-grandson practicing. You got talent, you know."

"Everybody says my dream is stupid. That playing soccer is not for mice."

"That's what they said to me too."

Louie's eyes opened wide. "You played soccer?"

The old mouse looked at the ground. "No." His voice sounded sad. "I listened to them. I let them talk me out of it. I've regretted it my whole life."

"Oh," Louie said. "I'm sorry."

"Don't let it happen to you. It doesn't matter what anyone says. It doesn't matter what anyone thinks of you. It doesn't matter if you're a hero or a fool or even if you're not good at it. It only matters that you pursue what you love with all your heart and try to become better."

Louie heard the school bell ring. He'd better hurry or he'd be late.

"I have to go," he said to the old mouse. "Thanks."

The mouse nodded and ducked into the shadows of the garbage can.

"Wait," Louie said. "What's your name?"

The old mouse poked his nose back into the light. "They call me Giresse."

"You mean like Alain Giresse, the star of the 1982 French team?"

The old mouse smiled and disappeared.

All through that school day, Louie's teachers had to remind him to pay attention. He kept thinking of his conversation with Giresse. He didn't want to give up what he loved like the old mouse had done.

Louie was still thinking about Giresse that evening when he and his parents and siblings crept to his Aunt Juliette's for a family dinner. Juliette lived in an apartment in the wall of a café in the train station. The floors rumbled with the comings and goings of the trains, but there were always good things to eat that Aunt Juliette had scrounged in the station.

The whole extended family of thirty-seven mice gathered around the big square table (an old pizza box turned upside down).

"Soccer's the greatest game in the world!" Louie told them once they began to eat.

His relatives all snorted or chuckled.

"Louie, forget about soccer," said his cousin Marcel. "If I were you, I'd concentrate on perfecting more traditional and practical mouse skills. You know, like gnawing and chewing and making nests."

Another cousin, Paul, who prided himself on being forward-thinking, said, "Louie, take my advice: learn a modern trade like plumbing or bookkeeping."

Louie scowled. Nobody understood his love for soccer. He didn't even understand it himself. But he remembered what Old Giresse had said, that it didn't matter what anyone thought of him, and he didn't respond to his cousins.

CHAPTER 5

"I will not lose my temper."

THE NEXT MORNING, Louie kicked his pea ball from the bedroom toward the kitchen. He dribbled around his brothers and sisters. They were scurrying about, getting ready for school.

"Louie, stop kicking that pea in the house!" his mother yelled for the millionth time.

"But *Maman*, I have to keep practicing, perfecting my touch on the ball."

"Not in this house, you don't!" she shouted, waving her wooden cooking spoon in the air for emphasis. "And not with my peas!"

Louie sighed. How would he ever make the French national team if he couldn't even practice in his own house?

Things were not any better at school. Later that morning, his teacher, Madame Lambert, caught him kicking his ball under his desk. “I warned you before, Louie, that if you didn’t put that pea away, I would have to take it from you.” She grabbed the ball and put it in the closet. She said she would return it to him after school, but during recess, Mean Manoche, a big bully of a mouse, stole the pea and ate it.

At lunchtime, Louie’s schoolmates laughed at him. “Louie the Loony, Louie the Loony,” they chanted.

“You’ll see,” François told the mice. “One day you’ll brag to everyone that you knew him before he got famous. Like Louie always says: ‘Where there’s a mouse, there’s a way.’”

“You mean,” Mean Manoche jeered, “that where there’s a Louie, there’s a shrimp.”

The other mice all squeaked with laughter.

“Take that back!” Louie yelled.

Mean Manoche sneered. “Make me.”

Louie leapt forward and tackled Manoche. The bully smelled like garlic and dried pea. He weighed twice as much as Louie.

They grappled on the ground while the other mice gathered around and chanted, “Fight! Fight! Fight!” Louie elbowed Manoche in the ribs, while Manoche tried pinning Louie’s arms to the ground.

Madame Lambert rushed over and separated them. “Louie, I’m disappointed in you,” she said. “I’ve told you before you must have better self-control.”

“But he started it,” Louie protested. “He called me a—”

“I don’t care what he called you. You can’t be fighting all the time.”

She made him stay late after school and write one hundred times on a piece of paper, *Je ne vais plus perdre mon calme*. “I will not lose my temper anymore.”

At the sixty-fifth line, Louie’s paw cramped. He wiggled it to loosen it up. Then he smiled as a funny idea came to him. He slipped in one line that read, *I will always fight back if someone makes fun of me*. He chuckled to himself and hoped that Madame Lambert wouldn’t notice. He knew that if she did, it would mean another

L'École

one hundred lines or something worse.

Louie finally finished, handed in his paper and rushed out the door before the teacher could discover line number sixty-six.

He found François waiting for him outside the school. A group of little mice were gathered at François' feet, listening to one of his stories as they often did after school.

"So then Little Red Riding Mouse said, 'What a big cheese you have, Grandma.'"

All the young mice giggled.

"Oh hi, Louie," François said. "Sorry kids; we'll finish the story tomorrow. Louie and I have to go practice now."

The little mice groaned.

François and Louie walked to the alley behind Louie's family's nest. Louie told François all about his encounter with Giresse.

François had never heard of the old mouse. "I like what he said, though, about pursuing what you love with all your heart and trying to become better."

They practiced kicking around a bit of an acorn until the sun was low in the sky and Louie's mother called to her children (in order of their age, as she always did). "Stuart, Bianca, Elizabeth, Martin, Bernard, Norman, Louie, come in now. It's time to eat your *soufflé au roquefort*."

After supper, Louie sneaked upstairs to where

the baker was watching a World Cup "friendly," an unofficial warm-up game, on television. France was playing Sweden. The Swedish team was strong and big, but they were no match for the nimble French players.

As he gazed at the screen from his hiding place beneath the creaky sofa, Louie particularly admired the play of Abidad Rouzon. The midfielder dribbled past opponent after opponent, and then placed perfect passes right to the feet or head of a teammate. He was a genius on the field.

When one of the Swedes cut Rouzon down from behind with a hard tackle, the baker and Louie both jumped to their feet at the same time.

The baker screamed, "Red card! Throw him out!"

Louie squeaked along with him. "Red card! Red card!"

The baker shook his fist and swore at the Swedish player.

Under the sofa, Louie shook his paw and hollered, "You oaf!"

The baker called to his wife, who was washing dishes in the kitchen. "Were you talking to me, *chérie*?"

"No, *chéri*," she called back.

Louie realized he'd better be quieter if he didn't want the baker to discover him. Like his mother said, humans could be unpredictable.

Just then, the camera panned to the French coach, Pierre Casparre, screaming at the referee. Casparre's face was red, and it looked like he was yelling some bad words. He had to be restrained by his more mild-mannered assistant coach, Henri Levi. Levi put his arm around Casparre, trying to calm him down.

Rouzon stood up and flexed his leg. He was OK. The crowd cheered. Rouzon quickly got revenge. He lofted the free kick right to the head of his teammate, Michel. Michel leapt up and put the ball neatly into the back of the net, giving France the winning goal. The victory added to the team's momentum on its way to the World Cup tournament.

When the game ended, the baker got up, humming the "Marseillaise," the French national anthem. He turned off the television and headed happily to bed.

Louie waited for the baker to leave the room. Then he crept down the stairs toward his own nest, humming the "Mouseillaise,"the national anthem of French mice.

That night, he dreamed that he was on the field playing with Rouzon and Michel and the rest of the French players, while Coach Casparre did cartwheels on the sidelines.

Early the next morning, François rushed into Louie's room. "Look at this!" he yelled, thrusting a torn piece of newspaper toward Louie's sleepy face. "This is the break you've been waiting for!"

CHAPTER 6

Scandal and Opportunity

LOUIE RUBBED HIS EYES. He remembered from his dream one perfect pass he had made to Michel that resulted in a goal.

The headline on the newspaper read, *Twelve Players Booted from French Squad in Betting Scandal. Coach Casparre to Conduct National Search for Replacements*. The article reported that Guy Gascon, the fast-living midfielder, along with eleven other French players, had been caught betting against their own team. This was a violation of international regulations. Casparre had no choice but to kick them off the squad.

The coaches were going to hold tryouts in a number of French cities, including Marseille.

"This is terrible!" Louie cried. "Those fools. They've ruined everything."

"Don't you get it, Louie? This is your chance! The Marseille tryout is in two days. Let's get to work."

A tryout! A genuine tryout with the national team. It was beyond Louie's dreams. Wait a second...What if he tried out and it went horribly? What if they all laughed at him? That would prove that everyone else was right, that his dream was stupid and he was an idiot. That he was "just a mouse." A pulse began throbbing in Louie's head.

"François," he said. "I've been thinking. Maybe I haven't tried hard enough to find other mice to play with. Maybe I should forget about playing with humans."

François stared at him. "You mean you're chickening out? You know there are no other mice to play with. You've been trying to do that for two years now. And I thought you really wanted to be a great soccer player."

"I do. But maybe I should start playing with a local human soccer club or something, or even human children, and get more experience, and not try to jump to the pros right off the bat. Maybe my father's right. It's too grandiose."

"Yes, you could try playing with humans, but that would probably take a while. This opportunity is staring you in the face right now," François said. "You can at least try out. What do you have to lose?"

My life, maybe, Louie thought. But he really *did* want to be a great soccer player. He remembered the sad look on Giresse's face. Louie gazed around his room. He saw the photos of soccer stars he had nibbled out of the newspaper and stuck to the wall. He saw his soccer cleats and clothing lying in a pile in the corner. He saw the latest pea resting on top of his jersey.

And trying out for the national team like this *was* a once in a lifetime opportunity. He swallowed hard. "OK, let's go." He climbed out of his tart-pan bed.

What was he getting himself into now?

François and Louie tried to imagine what kinds of tasks the coaches would have the players do at the tryouts. They practiced heading the ball, throw-ins, corner kicks, passing, defending.

At one point, to increase Louie's endurance, François climbed on his back and Louie did sprints while his friend shouted encouragement in his ear.

"Not so loud, please," Louie huffed as François' roly-poly belly pressed against his damp shirt.

Toward the end of the afternoon, Louie kicked the ball so hard that the pea shattered into sixteen pieces. Louie collapsed on the ground, panting, while François scampered around the grass, eating bits of the broken ball.

As they were walking home after practice, François had a thoughtful look on his face. "You know, if you really mean to play soccer with humans, you'll need to practice with a human-size ball. A dried pea is way too small."

"*Ah, bien, oui,*" said Louie, his heart sinking. A human regulation-size soccer ball would be about one hundred times his size. He had thought of this problem many, many times in the past and quickly shut it out of his mind each time. Now, he couldn't avoid the issue any more.

The next day, the day before the tryout, Louie and François crept down to the humans' elementary schoolyard a block away from their mouse school. Several boys and girls were playing soccer during recess. When the bell rang, the children scrambled inside and left the ball on the field.

Louie ran up to it and kicked it hard. "Ouch!" He hopped on one foot as he watched the ball roll a half inch along the grass.

"*Très bien*! You moved it!" cheered François.

Louie shook his head. His father was right. His dream was absurd. "This is crazy, François," he groaned.

"Of course it's crazy. Life is crazy. But the problem here," François continued, "is that you kicked the ball off-center. Given your size, you'll have to hit it exactly right, right in the sweet spot, to give it any juice. Try again."

Louie tried again. And again. And again, until his rear paws were sore. But he discovered that François was correct. If he kicked the ball in exactly the right spot, he could indeed make it move an inch or two. After one particularly well-placed kick, Louie smiled as the ball traveled three inches. Yes!

His smile faded. Three inches? That wouldn't be nearly good enough for the national team.

Following practice, François seemed satisfied, but Louie's stomach hurt. As tryout day dawned, he was no longer nervous. He was terrified. His whole body trembled as he imagined actually being on the same field with humans.

He realized it wasn't hard to have a dream, but it was hard to make the dream come true. He also knew he would never get another chance like this.

CHAPTER 7

At Stade Vélodrome

BY THE TIME THE TWO FRIENDS showed up at the Stade Vélodrome, the historic Marseille soccer stadium, Louie felt dizzy.

François looked at Louie with narrowed eyes. "Get a grip on yourself, mouse."

Louie recalled his brave words to his mother: "I will be the first mouse to play in the World Cup or I will get squished in the attempt." Now they didn't seem as inspiring as they had before.

"Today is Squish Day," he muttered to himself. He felt like he might throw up.

"What?" asked François.

"Wish Day. Today's Wish Day," said Louie.

François stared at him.

Louie cleared his throat. "Where do we go?"

They gazed up at the huge, gray stadium walls. Neither mouse had ever been in such a big structure before.

The stadium entrance area was deserted. They scooted under a locked metal gate and scurried down a dark corridor under the stands. Louie saw a man ahead sweeping the floor.

"We'll ask him," François said.

The man was listening to headphones as he worked and didn't seem to hear François shouting up to him. François jumped up and down and waved his paws to get the man's attention, but the worker still didn't notice the two mice at his feet.

Finally Louie went up to him and kicked his shoe.

The man jumped back, startled. "*Pardon*? What's this?" He took off the headphones.

"Louie's here for the tryouts," François explained. "Where should he go? Also, who's in charge of coordinating things? I'd like to speak with him."

The worker chuckled. "Mice playing soccer! Thank you. I needed a good laugh today."

Louie scowled at him.

"If you need to change your clothes, the locker room is that way. Be my guest." The man snickered and made a little bow to Louie. "And you," he said to François, "look for a bald man on the field with a clipboard. That's Monsieur LeMot, the team clerk."

"*Merci*," François said.

"*Pas du tout*," said the man.

Louie said nothing. He did not like people laughing at him.

The locker room was deserted. It smelled musty and sweaty. Louie's paws shook as he took his shorts and jersey out of his school backpack and pulled them on. But as soon as he put on his soccer cleats, his nervousness suddenly vanished and magically transformed into a joyful kind of energy. Just by being there, he'd already come farther than any other mouse in history. Louie did a cartwheel right there on the locker room bench. He'd give this tryout his best shot!

Louie jogged through a tunnel into the bright light and the green grass of the enormous soccer pitch. The playing field was gigantic. The goal posts at the far end of the pitch seemed vague and dreamlike in the distance. It was much, much larger than the field at the humans' elementary school.

He spotted François on the sideline, speaking with a man holding a clipboard. François' arms were waving and his face was red. Louie knew this meant his friend was upset.

Monsieur LeMot looked skeptical. "Where has he played before?" he asked, frowning.

"Lots of places!" cried François. "The park, the schoolyard, the street, the basement beneath the bakery—"

"I mean," the man interrupted, "for what teams has he played?"

"Just give me a chance," Louie said, jogging up. He clenched and unclenched his paws. The world was so unfair to mice.

The man's eyes opened wide. Apparently, he was surprised to see a mouse wearing soccer shorts and a soccer jersey. "I'm sorry, but we can't—" he started to say when another man walked up.

Louie recognized him from television as Henri Levi, the assistant coach.

"What do we have here?" asked Levi.

"This, uh, mouse, wants to try out for the team," Monsieur LeMot replied.

Levi knelt down on one knee so he was closer to Louie. "Have you been playing soccer for a long time?" he asked.

Louie thought Levi's eyes seemed kind. "Yes."

"And you think you're talented enough to make the national team?"

"Louie's the best soccer mouse in the whole world!" François shouted.

Monsieur Levi smiled. "You have a loyal friend there, Louie. Well, we'll see what you can do."

François and Louie cheered.

Monsieur LeMot had Louie sign a paper saying that if Louie got injured or squished, the French team would not be responsible. He told Louie to stretch and warm up and wait for the other players and coaches to arrive.

François, meanwhile, found a good seat in the first row of the stands. Louie spotted him scavenging peanuts that had been left on the ground at the club match the previous night.

Gradually, players started coming in. Lean, athletic-looking men ran onto the field and began kicking balls back and forth to each other. Tall men, short men, light-skinned, dark-skinned, some with long hair, some with shaved heads. They spoke French with all kinds of accents: Parisian, Arabic, Marseillais. All, even the shortest among them, were like giants to Louie.

Then everyone suddenly stopped whatever they were doing as onto the field jogged the stars of the French team: Michel and the goalie, Philipe, and the captain, Rouzon.

Louie never suspected *they* were going to show up. He was amazed to find himself on the same field as his heroes. He started to run toward Rouzon to ask for an autograph. He actually took a few steps before he regained control and retreated. "Steady, Louie, steady," he muttered to himself. "You're a player now, not a fan."

A whistle blew and there was Coach Casparre gesturing for everyone to gather round.

Louie scurried forward with the other players, careful to stay away from their feet. He didn't want to get squished before the tryout even began.

Coach Casparre opened his mouth and was about to begin speaking when Assistant Coach Levi whispered something to him and pointed at Louie.

Casparre seemed to notice Louie for the first time, and the other players did, too. Casparre's jaw stayed open, and he stared at Louie as if entranced. Finally he turned to Levi and bellowed, "Are you crazy? He's a mouse!"

The players guffawed.

Louie glared at them. He turned back to the coach. "Yes, I'm a mouse. That's obvious. And I'm also a soccer player and I deserve a chance. Please, Coach Casparre, let me have my chance."

"This is ridiculous!" the coach shouted. He turned to Levi. "Do you take me for a fool? Letting a mouse try out? What do you think this is, a circus? The theatre of the absurd? What do you think the press will say if they find out? I'll tell you what they'll say: '*Au revoir*, Casparre.' That's what they'll say!"

"Come on, Pierre. Let him have his chance," Levi said. "There's no press here. And it's not every day we get to see a mouse play the game. Besides, he has *chutzpah*, this mouse. I want to see what he's got."

"I can't argue with that," Casparre said. "The mouse certainly has nerve." He glared at Louie. "All right," he grumbled. "But don't blame me if they make mouse-meat out of you."

Louie gulped and gave François a thumbs-up.

CHAPTER 8

The Tryouts

THE TRYOUTS STARTED PRETTY WELL FOR LOUIE. In sprints up and down the field, he could keep up with and even run faster than some of the men. And his endurance was very good from all the practicing he had been doing.

From his place in the stands, François yelled encouragement.

"Go, Louie!"

"You can do it!"

"What a mouse! What a mouse!"

Then it came time to kick and receive the ball. Louie was not used to the speed and force with which these world-class players could kick the ball. One of the men passed the ball hard toward him. Without thinking, Louie jumped up to try to trap the pass with his chest. Oomff! He found himself lifted off his feet and flying, draped over the ball, across the field. "Aiiihhh!" he

screamed as he flew through the air. He landed on his butt far down the field.

Louie caught his breath and then felt his ribs and his backside. Everything seemed intact. He was OK, only a bit dizzy. He got up, brushed himself off, and ran back briskly for the next drill.

"I like your spirit, little one," Rouzon said as they took their places.

Louie blushed.

Louie noticed the coaches on the sideline pointing at him and whispering to each other. He knew he had been positioning himself in exactly the right spots during the flow of play. Could the coaches see that he had a great understanding of the game? Or were they concerned that his small size was preventing him from being more effective?

During one drill, Louie bravely leapt up to head the ball. Once again, the ball lifted him off his feet and sent him flying halfway down the field.

Rouzon ran to where Louie lay on his back, his head spinning. "Are you all right?"

"I'm fine. I'm fine," Louie said. The truth was he was embarrassed.

Rouzon burst out laughing.

All the other players began laughing too.

Louie glanced at the sideline and saw that even Casparre couldn't help smiling a bit.

Rouzon said, "Pardon me for laughing. It's only that you're so little, but you have such a big attitude. It's fantastic!"

Louie clenched his paws. But he took a breath and shrugged his shoulders and ran back to his position. He guessed it *was* kind of funny.

To Louie, it seemed that the rest of the tryouts went happily for the other players and coaches, if not for him. He thought that maybe his presence was lightening them up, causing them to relax. It seemed that Rouzon and Michel and Philipe were playing with even more joy than normal. At one point, Louie looked at the sideline again and saw Casparre and Levi gazing thoughtfully at him. He turned his attention back to the field as he tried to defend against a tall player on a corner kick.

Of course, Louie was about six feet too short, and the player easily jumped up and headed the ball toward the goal. Only a spectacular save by Philipe prevented a score.

Finally, the whistle blew, ending the tryout.

François ran up to Louie with a bottle cap full of water and a little towel. "Congratulations, Louie," he said, "You didn't get squished."

That's true, I guess, Louie thought. But he didn't score any goals. He couldn't stop the ball. He didn't make any passes. He couldn't defend. He couldn't really do anything but run. They'd never let him on the team now.

His shoulders slumped. He spit onto the grass. The more he thought about the tryout, the more he realized the whole thing had been a miserable failure.

Levi addressed everyone. "*Messieurs*, thank you for your efforts. We were impressed with each and every one of you, and we regret that we have only a few spots available on the roster. Will the following players please see Coach Casparre immediately?" He began reading off the names of the lucky winners in alphabetical order.

Louie did not expect to be selected. Nonetheless, his heart sank when Casparre passed the *Ls* in the alphabet and his name was not mentioned. He trudged off toward the sidelines, while the rest of the players, selected or not, remained on the field to stretch and chat.

What an idiot he was. His dream was absurd and stupid, and he was a fool to have ever imagined he could compete with humans. Casparre was right. His father was right. All his relatives and the mice in school were right. The library janitor was right. He was pathetic. A joke. A nothing. A nobody. Just a crummy mouse.

François patted his back, but Louie snarled, "Leave me alone, will you? Why don't you get your own life for a change instead of following me around all the time?"

François stood still.

Louie stormed into the locker room. He tore off his soccer cleats, threw them across the floor, and then broke down crying.

After a few minutes, François came in. He leaned against the door and stared at his friend. Louie wiped his eyes. He picked up his cleats, and without a word to each other, the two mice walked out of the room and started making their way toward the stadium exit.

Finally, Louie spoke. "I'm sorry for what I said about you back there."

François nodded.

"You're right, François. I did the best I could. I just wasn't good enough. Same as most of the guys who tried out today." He almost felt proud of himself for having the courage to have given it his best shot.

Right before they reached the outside gate, someone ran up to them. "Monsieur LaSurie, wait a moment." It was Coach Levi. He was panting. "Thank goodness I caught you before you left. Coach Casparre and I were talking. We admire your spunk and your desire. It's unfortunate there is not presently a mouse league, as we are sure you would be a star in it."

"Thank you very much, Monsieur Levi," Louie muttered and continued walking. He did not want Levi to feel sorry for him.

"Wait," Levi commanded.

Louie turned around.

"Coach Casparre and Captain Rouzon and I all feel that you would be a valuable addition to the team, not as a player, but as an assistant coach. Your presence makes the players happy and seems to inspire them. With the betting scandal and all, we need a lift and we think you can provide one. What do you say?"

"I am a soccer player, not a mascot," Louie said. He snorted. *I don't want to be a cheerleader. I want to play the game!*

"*Non, non, pas du tout*," said Levi. "You misunderstand me."

"What do you mean then?"

"You seem to have a great knowledge of soccer. Coach Casparre and I would like you to serve as our assistant, giving us advice from your unique perspective, so to speak, and also to be in charge of the *esprit de corps* of the players."

Louie stared blankly at Levi. Finally, he noticed François' elbow in his ribs. François was nodding at him to say something.

"Uh, what would I do, exactly?"

"You'd be present at all practices and games. You'd watch the players and take notes on their body alignment and positioning on the field. Your sharp eyes can see details that Casparre and I might miss. And you'd meet with us and plan strategy.

"Oh in that case," Louie said to Levi, still dazed, "I'd love to."

"*Fantastique*!" said François.

"Wonderful," exclaimed Levi. "We'll get you a train ticket to Paris. You can stay at my apartment with me and my family for the six weeks until the tournament is over. And you can drive to all the practices with me."

Levi reached down and they shook hands.

As soon as Louie and François walked out of the stadium and were out of sight, they whooped and hugged and jumped up and down.

"Yes! Yes! Yes!" Louie screamed.

"You're a coach!" François shouted. "You're a coach of *les Bleus*!"

They bounced up and down for a long time, and then finally, when they had calmed down a little, they headed to the metro.

Tucked under a bench in a corner of the train car to avoid the feet and eyes of the commuters, the two friends rode back home. They discussed the tryout in great detail, talking fast because they were so excited. They couldn't believe Louie's good fortune. Not only did he survive the experience without serious injury, but he was actually invited to assist the team.

He would be the first mouse in the world to help coach a World Cup soccer team, or for that matter, any soccer team.

"This is really great, François," Louie said. "I'll learn so much about the game. But you know, I still want to *play* soccer, not just coach it."

"Be patient, Louie," François counseled. "I have a feeling you'll get your chance sooner or later."

"I hope so." Louie's face suddenly went pale. "Oh no!"

"What?"

"My mother. What will she say when I tell her I've been hired by the national team and need to go to Paris for six weeks? She's scared to even let me go around the corner by myself, let alone to Paris. If she says no, it's all ruined."

Louie wrung his paws. This was a problem. A big problem.

CHAPTER 9

Farewell to Marseille

"ABSOLUTELY NOT!" Louie's mother stood in the kitchen, whipping her soufflé faster and faster. "Paris is too dangerous."

"Marseille is dangerous, too," Louie said. "More than Paris, even." His heart was beating as fast as his mother's whisk was whipping. Everything depended on his convincing her to let him go.

"He's right about that," Louie's father said. "Marseille is dangerous, too."

Louie nodded and held his breath.

Louie's mother glanced sharply at his father and then turned back to Louie. "And what about school? You can't miss so much school."

Louie was ready for this argument. "This will be a great education," he replied. "I'm sure I'll learn more than I would just going to school. And it's only for six weeks. Madame Lambert can give me assignments so

I can keep up."

"Yes," Louie's father, who had never been a very good student himself, added, "this will be a great educational opportunity." Ever since Louie had told his father about the offer to coach, his father had been very excited about the possibility.

"Coach Levi will meet me at the train station. And I'll be living at his house. It's not like I'll be all alone in Paris. I'll be safe. Please, *Maman*?"

Madame LaSurie looked from Louie to her husband and back again. Both of them were staring at her expectantly.

"All right." She sighed. "Just don't get squished."

Louie and his father cheered, and Louie rushed up and kissed his mother.

Two days later, Louie was to depart for Paris and the headquarters of the French team. His mother made him check that he had packed all the things he would need as assistant coach: stopwatch, clipboard, pens and pencils, plus a peanut butter sandwich for lunch on the train, sunflower seeds for a snack, and a cheese cupcake for dessert.

Finally it was time to head to the train station. "Stay away from cats and rats," she advised him. "And don't trust every mouse you meet, either."

"I *know.*" Louie fiddled with his tail and checked his pocket one more time to make sure he had his train reservation. He wished he wasn't so nervous.

But wouldn't any young mouse heading to Paris to serve as assistant coach of the national team be nervous?

His mother kissed Louie and immediately burst into tears.

Louie was surprised to find tears flowing from his eyes, too. They trickled down his whiskers and plopped onto the floor. "Pull yourself together, mouse," Louie urged himself.

He wiped his eyes and turned to his father.

Monsieur LaSurie looked at Louie, pounded his back and said, "I knew you could do it, son."

Louie couldn't remember a single time his father had thought he could do it before three days ago. "Thanks, Papa," he said.

Louie hugged each of his four brothers and two sisters.

There was a knock at the door of their nest. François was there to walk with Louie to the train station. Louie had tried to persuade Levi to allow François to come with him to Paris, but Levi said the team budget did not allow it. Plus, François' parents would never let him miss so much school.

"I wish you were going with me, François," Louie said.

"Yeah, me too. Write me, OK?"

"Of course," Louie said.

It was a fine spring morning in Marseille. The sun felt good on Louie's face. A mild breeze stirred the short hairs on top of his head. The two friends discussed the French team's chances at the World Cup and who the favorites were to win the tournament. Italy would be tough as usual. Brazil was certain to be strong. Germany, England, Spain and the Ivory Coast all had very good teams, too.

When they walked by the garbage can where he had talked with Giresse, Louie looked around for the old mouse. There was no sign of him. Had he imagined Giresse? Louie had not seen him since that one morning.

"Psst, Shortie!"

Louie jerked his head around.

There was Giresse on the sidewalk behind him. His bleary eyes seemed to glow with excitement. "Glad I caught you before you left."

François's mouth dropped open.

"I got some advice for you, Shortie," the old mouse croaked. "Be ready for anything."

Louie nodded. "*Merci*, Monsieur Giresse."

"And for you, DuBois, I hear you're a good storyteller. Keep it up. The world needs your stories."

Before Louie or François could say anything, the mouse slipped back into a shadow and disappeared.

"He's a strange old guy," François said. "But I like him."

"Yeah," Louie said. "Me too. I'm glad you got to meet him."

When they arrived at the station, humans were everywhere, walking quickly with great determination. Some pulled suitcases on wheels. With perfect timing, Louie and François jumped onto one of the suitcases and rode it, unnoticed, all the way to the ticket booth. It was a bumpy ride, but exhilarating.

Louie was now an employee of the French national team and had an official reservation. He was relieved that for the first time in his life, he would not need to sneak onto a train.

Louie and François jumped off the suitcase. Louie rubbed his tail, which had gotten a little cramped during the ride. He shimmied up the side of the ticket booth. He stood on the counter in front of the ticket window.

When she saw Louie, the thin, pinched woman behind the window waved her hands and said in a shrill voice, "Shoo! Shoo! Go away, you mouse!"

"I have a reservation," Louie said. He showed it to her and asked where to go to catch his train.

She looked at it carefully and then back at Louie. Then she scowled and printed out his ticket and pointed the way to his train platform.

After some searching, Louie and François found the right train. It was time to say goodbye. "I'll get you some game tickets if I can," Louie promised.

"Thanks, Louie," François said. "I'll miss our practice sessions."

"Me too," Louie responded, a lump in his throat. "I couldn't have done it without you."

The train whistle blew. François and Louie hugged goodbye. Louie hoisted up his little trunk and got on board.

Louie found his seat and climbed to the top. No one was sitting next to him. From his perch, he looked through the window and waved to François, who waved back to him from the platform.

The train began moving, taking Louie toward his new life as a World Cup coach.

Louie enjoyed the first part of the trip to Paris. He studied his notes, ate his sandwich, his snack, and his cupcake, and looked out the window. *The world is sure a big place*, he thought, as farms and towns and woods rolled by. Occasionally, the train passed people playing soccer in a field or a backyard or schoolyard, and Louie craned his neck to watch them before they drifted out of sight. He sighed. Some day, he hoped, he'd get to play in an actual game. After a while, he scooted down onto the seat and dozed.

The only scary part of the trip came when the train stopped at Lyon to let passengers off and on. A heavyset woman got on board. Apparently, she didn't realize Louie's seat was taken, and that Louie was, in fact, curled up in a ball, sleeping on it.

Louie looked up just in time to see her enormous backside descending toward him.

He leaped out of the way, narrowly avoiding getting squashed. He cleared his throat politely to get her attention, but she didn't seem to hear him. So he poked her in the leg with one of his pencils.

She did not appear happy to see a mouse next to her, but when Louie explained the situation and showed her his ticket, she said, "Hmph," got up, and found another seat.

When the train finally pulled into the Paris station, Louie retrieved his trunk from under the seat, waited until the other passengers had departed, and jumped off the train. Louie looked around for Coach Levi, who was supposed to meet him on the platform. Louie didn't see Levi anywhere.

Louie's heart started racing. He stared all around. The Marseille station was big, but this one was bigger and noisier and more chaotic. There were more humans in one place than Louie had ever seen before.

He waited on the platform. For ten minutes. Twenty minutes. Thirty minutes. With each passing minute, Louie's stomach clenched tighter and tighter.

Then the thought hit him. He was alone and abandoned in Paris!

CHAPTER 10

Louie in Paris

LOUIE TOOK A FEW DEEP BREATHS to calm himself. Unsure what to do next, he began lugging his trunk toward the central waiting area. Maybe he had misunderstood, and Levi was going to meet him there and not on the platform.

Honk! A horn blared behind him. It was a baggage cart speeding right at him! Louie leapt out of the way, avoiding the cart's huge wheels by inches.

As he hit the ground, Louie's trunk burst open and the contents spread out onto the platform. "*Imbécile*!" he yelled at the driver as the cart receded into the distance.

Louie shoved his clothes back in his trunk, muttering all the while. When he finished, he looked up and his eyes grew wide. Two mice were leaning against a post, pointing at him and snickering. One of them was tall and skinny and was wearing a jaunty black beret. The other was smoking a cigarette.

"Judging by your accent," the taller one said, "you are from Marseille. Am I correct?"

"Yes."

"And what brings such a nice young mouse as yourself to our lovely City of Lights, may I ask?"

"I'm going to be assistant coach of the National soccer team."

The two other mice looked at each other and burst out laughing.

"It's true," Louie insisted.

"No need to get upset," the shorter one said, stubbing out his cigarette. "It's only that we've never heard that one before. And we've heard everything."

"Well, there's never been a mouse soccer coach before," Louie said. "I'm the first one."

"That certainly deserves a celebration, don't you think, Pascal?"

"Of course it does, Laurent." The tall mouse took Louie's arm. "And you, our young friend from Marseille, must join us."

"But I'm supposed to meet Coach Levi. He said—"

"Well he's not here is he?" said Pascal. "Looks like he abandoned you."

"Maybe somebody's playing a big joke on you," Laurent said. "Who ever heard of a mouse coaching soccer?"

A painful doubt gnawed in Louie's mind. What if they were right?

"Yes," Pascal said, still holding tightly onto Louie's arm. "You must come with us. We insist."

Louie remembered his mother's words about not trusting every mouse he met. These two did not seem trustworthy.

"I'm sorry but I can't."

Laurent grabbed Louie's other arm. "But you must."

Laurent's grip was very strong.

"Let go!" Louie cried. He twisted his body and jerked out of Laurent's grip and then out of Pascal's. He picked up his trunk and hurried off down the platform.

The two mice scooted after him.

Just then, Louie spied Coach Levi rushing down the platform toward him. Jogging to keep up with Levi was a girl about eleven years old.

"Louie, there you are!" shouted Levi.

Louie looked back over his shoulder. Laurent and Pascal had disappeared.

"I'm sorry we were so late," Levi said. "We got caught in a terrible traffic jam. You must have been worried."

"*Pas de problème*," Louie said. "It's fine." He held his twitching tail in his paw so Levi wouldn't see how relieved he was that the coach had shown up.

Louie shook hands with Levi.

"Louie, this is my daughter, Rose," the man said.

"Nice to meet you," Louie said.

"I'll carry your trunk," the girl said. "And you can ride on my shoulder if you want."

Louie hopped up, and together the man, girl, and mouse made their way through the station to the street. It was fun riding on the girl's shoulder, although her long brown hair tickled his nose.

They found Levi's car, and Louie rode into the streets of Paris with his new friends. Louie wondered about the challenges awaiting him. Would he get lost in the big city? Would he be any good as a coach? Would the players take him seriously? He chewed his whiskers, pondering these questions. Like Old Giresse had said, he better be ready for anything.

CHAPTER 11

A New Home

ON THE WAY TO LEVI AND ROSE'S apartment, Louie caught glimpses of famous Paris landmarks. "There's the Eiffel Tower!" he yelled. "There's the Seine!" Suddenly his face grew warm. "You must think I'm a silly mouse from the sticks," he said to Rose.

"Oh, not at all," she replied. "Papa told me all about you. I think you're the most marvelous mouse in the whole world."

Louie turned and looked out the window so she would not see him blush through his fur.

They arrived at Levi's cluttered but cozy apartment. It was on the second floor of an old building in the Le Marais district of Paris.

Levi introduced Louie to his wife, Rochelle, a cheerful woman with a big smile. "This is Louie LaSurie, our new assistant coach."

"You must be starved after your long trip," she said to Louie.

Louie did not argue, even though he had had plenty to eat on the train.

"Well, dinner will be ready soon. Rose, please show Louie his room."

Louie's room was a corner of a closet in Rose's bedroom. Rose had prepared a shoebox filled with an old purple scarf as a bed. "I hope you like it," she said.

"I love it," Louie replied.

That night, when he and Rose were each in their own beds, and the lights were turned off, they chatted. Louie lay with both of his arms crossed behind his head and his feet stretched in front of him. "I can't believe that only this morning, I was in Marseille."

"What's Marseille like, Louie? I've always wanted to go there."

"Parts of it are really tough. But there are a lot of fun places, too. Like the Mouse-Go-Round and the Ferret's Wheel. And it's beautiful near the sea. Marseille is dangerous for mice, of course, but every place is dangerous for us."

"I'm sorry," Rose said.

"It's just the way things are. Maybe some day you can visit me there and I'll show you around."

"That would be great."

Eventually, Louie got too sleepy to talk anymore. Thinking about Marseille made him homesick. He fell asleep in his new bed and dreamed of home.

When he woke up the next morning, Louie's stomach was tense with anticipation of starting his new job. But he had the morning off before his coaching work began. Rose suggested they go on an adventure to help him relax. She found a toy bicycle that belonged to one of her dolls that was exactly the right size for a mouse.

Louie had never ridden a bicycle before, but after a few wobbly loops around the bedroom and one or two falls, he quickly got the hang of it. He rang the bicycle's tiny bell over and over again until Rose asked him to please stop.

He and Rose headed outside on their bikes to explore the neighborhood. Louie wore a little backpack in which he kept a water bottle and a raisin for a snack. It was a lovely May morning. They stayed on the sidewalk in order to avoid cars and buses. Louie rode behind Rose when it was crowded, and when there were fewer people on the sidewalk, they rode side by side. Louie had to pedal hard to keep up with her.

Louie kept his eyes out for cats or dogs who might like nothing more than to chase a mouse, whether that mouse was on a bicycle or on foot. But as long as Rose was with him, Louie felt safe.

Many of the pedestrians turned and stared and pointed when they saw the girl and the mouse bicycling together down the street. Louie waved to them and rang his bell jauntily. He almost forgot about the huge coaching challenge that awaited him.

Rose pointed out her school, the apartment where her best friend, Amie, lived, the place where she once found a ten-euro bill on the ground by a tree, the soccer field where her team played, and other notable landmarks.

At one point, Louie challenged Rose to a race. He was in fantastic shape from all his soccer training, and his little legs pumped up and down at a furious pace.

Rose was faster, however, and she beat him to the streetlamp that marked the end of their racecourse.

They rested there, panting and laughing.

They turned around to head back home. Rose gradually pulled away from him as Louie gazed around at the many sights on the busy street. Then Louie heard the rapid click of paws on the sidewalk behind him. He looked over his shoulder. A French bulldog with a mushed-in face was running right toward him. The dog's eyes were narrowed in a mean kind of way that made Louie's stomach flip.

Rose was a half block ahead.

Louie tried to call her, but his voice wasn't loud enough to be heard over the noise of the traffic. Louie stood up on the pedals to go faster. But it was no use. In a few more seconds, the dog would be upon him!

CHAPTER 12

Coach LaSurie

LOUIE SWERVED THE BIKE SHARPLY TO THE LEFT. The rear tire swung around fast and the bike tilted toward the ground. The sidewalk suddenly filled Louie's field of vision. "I'm going to crash!" his mind screamed. But at the last minute he righted the bike and zipped off again. Sweat trickled down between his shoulder blades.

The bulldog couldn't turn so fast. He tried to follow Louie, but stumbled over his own feet and crashed to the sidewalk, yelping.

Louie noticed an open door to a butcher shop and careened on his bicycle right into the shop.

The dog ran after him, barking furiously, but a man in a white apron shooed the dog away down the block. The man apparently had not noticed that a mouse had already entered the store.

Louie darted out of the store and spotted Rose on the

sidewalk. She had a panicked expression on her face. He cried, "Here I am!"

Rose's face brightened. "Oh, Louie, you gave me a scare."

Now that he was safe, Louie tottered a little. He took a drink of water to calm down. He told Rose about his escape as they rode home. Louie decided not to mention the incident with the bulldog to his mother.

That afternoon, after the excitement of his escape from the dog, a different kind of excitement started. Louie's coaching duties began. He and Levi and Head Coach Casparre had to prepare the new players and get everyone gelling together as a team. The tournament started in only three weeks. They didn't have much time.

The three coaches met in Casparre's office to discuss the best placement and combination of players. The two men sat on chairs around a table, and Louie sat on a box of matches on top of the table. It was a little scratchy on his bottom.

"I say we go with a single striker up top and support him with a solid midfield," Casparre said.

That's dumb, Louie thought. He opened his mouth a couple of times to share his observations, but then closed it before speaking. It was his very first day and he didn't want to contradict Casparre.

But then Levi asked him, "Louie, you've been quiet so far. What do you think would be our best formation?"

"I think we'd be fools to play with only one striker,"

Louie said. "It's too negative, too defensive. Michel needs more support up top."

"Are you calling me a fool?" Casparre snapped.

Louie cringed. "No, that's not what I meant. I just think we need to be more focused on attacking."

"We'd only be opening ourselves up for trouble," Casparre countered.

"I think Louie may have a point, Pierre," said Levi. "Our back line is solid. We have confidence in them. But we do need more firepower up front if we want to score goals. What do you think about going with four defenders, four midfielders, and two forwards?"

"A 4-4-2? Ridiculous!" shouted Casparre.

"What's ridiculous about it?" yelled Levi.

"Three mids and three forwards would be even better," interjected Louie. "We have the talent to pull it off."

Soon all three coaches were shouting and pacing,

their hands gesturing wildly. Louie got so caught up in the argument, he forgot to be shy. To make his case, Louie pounded his paw on the table. Ouch! He rubbed his paw and hoped Levi and Casparre hadn't noticed him wince.

Finally, after arguing for an hour, Casparre surprised Louie by saying suddenly, "Good conversation, gentlemen. Lots of food for thought here. Let's sleep on it." He wasn't angry at Louie. He just seemed to like to argue.

Louie was beginning to understand the head coach's temperament and style.

The next morning, Coach Levi introduced Louie to the players.

Several of them snickered. One player said, "A mouse is our coach? What's next? A cockroach?"

Louie felt all the blood rush to his head. A cockroach? That was worse than being called a shrimp.

Before Louie could think of a come-back, another player said, "A moth?"

Someone else said, "An ant?"

The team was really getting into this now.

"A flea?"

With the mention of each new insect, the players laughed harder.

Louie's pulse rose, and he felt the familiar flooding of anger and shame. *Don't cry. Don't cry*, he told himself. He took a deep breath and walked right up to one of the wise guys. "Your job, I believe, is to play soccer, not to criticize the coaching staff. Is that correct, Coach Levi?"

Levi smiled. "Absolutely correct, Coach LaSurie." He stared at the players. "I encourage every one of you to remember that if you intend to remain part of this team."

Yeah, you tell 'em! Louie thought. It felt good to be supported like this.

Over the course of the next few days, the players gradually seemed to realize that their new coach was tough but fair and had a great knowledge of the game. Maybe they were starting to accept him.

For example, one hot afternoon while Louie was timing the players doing sprints, one of the new team members complained about the drill. "C'mon Coach," he said to Louie, "it's too hot. Ease up on us a little."

Louie stared at him. "Do you think the Italians are going to 'ease up' on you?" he said. "Do you think Brazil is going to 'ease up' on you? Run, don't whine! *Allez, allez*, go, go!"

Later Louie gave a suggestion to another of the players. "Gerard, try adjusting the angle of your ankle when you kick the ball. Flex it inward about five degrees. I think you'll find you have a lot more power and accuracy." Louie drew a picture of an ankle on his clipboard to show what he meant.

The player tried it and then gaped at the mouse in amazement as the ball sailed far down the pitch. "Coach," he said to Louie, "you're a genius!"

"No way. I'm just someone who sees things close up. You would too, if you were my size." Louie was thrilled. He hadn't been sure his suggestion would work for a human.

Louie soon became a popular figure in the locker room and on the field. When things got tense, as they often did under the pressures of preparing for the tournament, Louie would mimic great players of the past and get the team laughing and joking once again.

His imitation of Maradona's controversial goal in the 1986 World Cup was especially popular. The mouse leapt up as if he were heading an imaginary ball and then raised his paw next to his head and struck it forward, just like the Argentinian star did when he hit the ball into the goal with his hand, not his head. That incident has been referred to ever since as "The Hand of God."

"It's the Paw of God!" Michel shouted.

"Do it again, Louie," urged Gerard.

Louie loved performing. Maybe when his soccer career was over, he'd become an actor.

"He brings us good luck," yelled Philipe, the goalie, after France defeated Portugal 4-1 in the final pre-tournament friendly match a week after Louie's arrival in Paris.

Everything was going well. But Louie knew that the French team would soon need more than mere luck if they hoped to advance beyond the first round of the tournament. They'd have to play with as much skill and courage as possible.

CHAPTER 13

Never-Before-Seen Dribbling

AS MUCH AS LOUIE ENJOYED COACHING, he did miss playing the game himself. So in the evenings, he and Rose kicked a ball back and forth. Rose was a very skilled player and was a star midfielder on her youth team. Sometimes they played with a dried-pea ball on the floor in Rose's room. Louie kicked the pea with his feet and Rose flicked it back to him with her finger. And sometimes they went outside and played with a regulation ball in the courtyard behind Rose's apartment.

One evening, when they were playing outside, Rose passed the ball to Louie fast and hard. He wouldn't be able to stop it. He'd be bowled over. Louie remembered what that felt like from the tryout.

"Yaahh!" Louie yelled as he leapt straight up, out of the way of the onrushing ball. He landed right on the top of it. The ball's rotation immediately threw him off onto the brown dirt of the courtyard. He lay on the ground without moving.

Rose rushed up to him. "Are you OK?"

"I was just thinking," Louie said. Maybe, by moving his rear legs fast enough to maintain his balance, he could stay on the ball without falling off. He got back to his feet. "Kick it hard to me again."

Rose kicked the ball, and Louie tried jumping on top once more. This time, he managed to remain on it for a couple of seconds before tumbling to the ground.

He tried over and over. Louie discovered that if he started his feet running before he even landed on the ball, he could keep his balance. And if he pumped his arms hard enough and kicked with his feet, he could actually propel the ball forward. The faster he ran on top of the ball, the faster it moved. And by shifting his weight, he could direct the ball toward the left or right.

Rose clapped her hands and jumped up and down. "You're doing it, Louie. You're doing it!"

Louie fell off many times while perfecting this technique. Running on the ball made him a little dizzy, and all the falling was bending his whiskers and making his clothes very dusty. But each time he tumbled to the ground, he would laugh and say, "Let's try again."

After several days of practice, and much falling, Louie perfected this never-before-seen manner of playing soccer. Rose could pass the ball as hard as she wanted to him. He would time his leap perfectly, land on top of the ball, already running in place on his hind legs, with his arms pumping vigorously. It was the most fun Louie ever had. His body felt at one with the ball.

By leaning and twisting his body, Louie was able to maneuver the ball with precision. When he ran really fast, the ball moved very quickly, and even Rose had a hard time keeping up with him. Louie rode the ball up and down the courtyard at surprising speed, back and forth, zigging and zagging. He loved the feel of the spinning ball under his cleats and the way the wind rushed through his fur and whiskers as he steered it around the yard.

Rose set up an obstacle course of stones and sticks. She borrowed a stopwatch from her father and timed Louie. After three days of practice, Louie could make it through the course with his new technique almost as fast as Rose could by dribbling with her feet in the more traditional soccer method.

"You're a speed demon, Louie!" Rose shouted.

"I wish I had discovered this way of playing before the Marseille tryout." Louie sighed. "Ah, but it probably wouldn't have made a difference in me getting on the team."

"I'm glad you're the coach," Rose said. "We get to play together more this way."

"That's true. Anyway, no use worrying about what might have been, right?" he said, trying to convince himself.

Each night, Louie wrote letters to François and his family. He told them all about the players and Rose and his new method of dribbling a regulation ball and the meals Madame Levi had prepared that day. Writing to them made him realize how much he missed them and missed home. At the same time, he was excited and grateful to be part of this big adventure, and to be making new friends like Rose and Levi and Rouzon.

On the day before the month-long tournament began, the team had the day off to rest. Louie went with Rose that afternoon to watch her youth team practice. Louie stood on the sidelines under a small umbrella. Rose was a fearless athlete. She played with an intensity that impressed Louie. If any ball came her way, she was determined to win it, even if the other girls were bigger and stronger than her. They couldn't match Rose's resolve and determination.

"You inspire me," Louie told her as they rode their bikes home after practice.

"Thanks, Louie. And you inspire *me*. You never give up. And you always have good ideas."

Louie hoped that was true. The French team might need his ideas. The World Cup was set to begin.

CHAPTER 14

Opening Ceremonies

DESPITE THE BETTING SCANDAL and the rearrangement of their team, the French players' hopes were high during the opening ceremonies.

Louie marched onto the field of the magnificent national stadium in Paris, the Stade de France, along with the rest of the French squad. He stayed aware of the tromping feet near him, even as he gazed around, awed by the colorful crowd packed into the stands. It wouldn't do to get stepped on right at the outset of the tournament.

Louie couldn't help grinning as he walked. Then he spotted a close-up of himself on the huge stadium video screen. It showed him marching next to his human teammates.

Soon people were pointing and yelling, snapping photos and craning their necks to get a better view of the small French coach. Before long, the entire crowd was on its feet, laughing and yelling and cheering the mouse. He had become an instant celebrity. Louie glanced at Casparre. The head coach seemed surprised by the commotion Louie had caused. They had been so focused on preparing the team, they hadn't braced themselves for this kind of reaction to Louie.

Louie imagined his family and François back home in Marseille.They weren't able to get off work and be excused from school to come to Paris. At that very moment, they'd be watching and rooting for him from their viewing spot under the baker's sofa. His body felt warm as he thought of how proud his family must be of him. He wondered if Giresse was watching somewhere, too.

After the opening ceremony, journalists from around the world pressed closer to interview the new French assistant coach.

Louie fidgeted, not used to being the center of so much attention.

"Monsieur LaSurie," a reporter from Mali asked him in French, "Do you believe France can advance out of the first round, given the loss of so many players recently?"

Louie gazed nervously at the many microphones pointed down toward him. He took a deep breath. "First round? We'll be going to the semifinals, if not further."

Some of the journalists laughed at this bold prediction. "You really think France is as good as Brazil,

Germany, and the other great teams here?" a British writer asked in English.

"Yes I do, and here is why..." Louie proceeded to provide a detailed analysis of the various teams'

prospects, their strengths and weaknesses.

An American reporter asked Louie how it was possible that he, as a mouse, was able to become assistant coach. Louie told the man his favorite saying, "Where there's a mouse, there's a way."

The next day, Levi brought newspapers from all around the world to the breakfast table. They showed Louie's photograph with the caption beneath it repeating his motto.

Le Monde, Paris, France:
"*Avec une souris, tout est possible*."
The Sun, London, England:
"Where there's a mouse, there's a way."
Bild, Berlin, Germany:
"*Wo eine Maus ist, ist auch ein Weg*."
La Gazzetta Dello Sport, Milan, Italy:
"*Dove c'è un topo, c'è una maniera*."
The Jerusalem Post, Jerusalem, Israel:
"איפה שיש עכבר, יש דרך!"
Renmin Ribao, Beijing, China:
"只要有老鼠, 就有方法"
El País, Madrid, Spain:
"*Donde hay un ratón, hay una manera*."
Al Ahram, Cairo, Egypt:
"أين الماوس هناك طريقة"
Folha De Sao Paulo, Brazil:
"*Onde há um camundongo, há uma maneira*."

Louie carefully cut out the articles to put in his scrapbook. He couldn't wait to show them to François and his family.

At the same time, a nagging voice spoke in his head. "This is all fine," it said, "but you're not doing what you really want to do – play the game." *Will you shut up?* Louie thought. But he knew the voice was correct. He still wanted to play, more than anything. Would he ever get his chance?

CHAPTER 15

Close Call

THE DAY AFTER THE OPENING CEREMONIES, Louie went with Rose to her school. The principal had invited the mouse to give a speech to the students. Louie's stomach hurt. Schools made him nervous. The smell of a school reminded him of tests and assignments and being scolded by teachers.

Plus he was not used to giving speeches. "I don't have anything to say," he complained to Rose as they rode their bikes to the school. "What if I freeze up? What if I lose my voice? I've heard of that before, 'stress-induced laryngitis.' What if my pants fall down while I'm talking? What if—"

"Calm down, Louie," Rose said. "Your pants are not going to fall down. You're not going to lose your voice."

Easy for you to say, Louie thought. *You're not the one whose pants are at risk here*.

For some reason he was not that scared talking to

grown-up reporters or soccer players or the other coaches, but the prospect of speaking to children terrified him.

In the auditorium, Louie stood on top of the front edge of a lectern, facing the students. Two hundred children of many different races and backgrounds all stared up at him, whispering and pointing. His paws were sweaty as he held his notes. He spoke into a microphone twice as big as his own head. "It's my great honor to stand before you today. I—"

He was interrupted by a screech of feedback as the microphone was turned up louder so everyone could hear him.

"Sorry," the principal said sheepishly in the corner, adjusting the audio controls.

"It's my great stand to honor before you today," Louie began again.

Everyone laughed.

"I mean it's my great today to honor your stand."

Everyone laughed even harder.

Louie blushed. He fumbled with his notes, and they slipped out of his paws. He watched them float to the floor far below. He thought of scooting down to retrieve them, but it was a long way down and back, and he decided to simply forget about the notes.

"Look," he began again. "I'm not used to giving speeches. I'm not even used to being around so many humans. I grew up in a hole in a wall beneath a bakery in Marseille."

Some of the students tittered.

"How many of you have ever been to Marseille?"

About a dozen children raised their hands.

"I was the only mouse who liked soccer. And lots of mice made fun of me because of it. I didn't like being teased all the time – they called me 'Louie the Loony'— but I wasn't going to give up."

Louie proceeded to tell the students how he tried out for the national team and got selected to be assistant coach and traveled to Paris and became friends with Rose. Then he wasn't sure what to say, so he said, "Um, uh, OK. Study hard, children, and always listen to your teachers."

Louie saw Rose grimace in the front row. He realized how lame this advice sounded. Also, he felt like a hypocrite. The truth was that he had never studied particularly hard, nor was he known for listening to his teachers. But it seemed like the responsible thing for a mouse in his position to say during a speech in a school auditorium.

"Even more important than studying hard is to never bully anyone just because they seem different than you or weaker or smaller." He saw the teachers and some of the kids nodding their heads in agreement.

"Most importantly," he said, finally warming up to his talk, "hold fast to what you love. An old mouse told me this once: if you love something, devote yourself to it with all your heart. Study it. Practice. Dream. It doesn't matter what anyone says or thinks about your dream. If you love it, you must pursue it. You *must!* There *is* a way…Even if you're not a mouse."

Everyone laughed and cheered.

Rose beamed.

Louie hopped down to the flat part of the lectern and shimmied down the lectern's leg to the floor, relieved that the speech was over.

A number of the students crowded around him to shake his paw, say hello and ask for his autograph.

Louie looked up from signing his name to see a boy reaching down toward him. Before Louie could dart out of the way, the boy grabbed his tail. The boy ran out of the hall, dangling Louie upside down in front of him.

"You're giving bullies a bad name, *Louie the Loony*," the boy sneered. "That's why I'm throwing you down the toilet."

Louie had never learned to swim. "Let me go!" he cried. "Let me go!" He thrashed and squirmed, but couldn't free himself. He was dizzy from hanging upside down.

Rose came sprinting after the boy. She leaped and tackled him around the ankles.

Louie heard the boy's chin smacking the ground.

Louie flew out of his grasp and slid along the waxed floor. He tried desperately to keep his balance, like a speed skater who had lost control. Louie's paws flailed

wildly. His eyes got wide as he saw the wall approaching fast. He leaned far to the left and fell on his side. The friction of his clothes on the floor slowed him down so he only bumped against the wall instead of crashing into it.

Rose picked up Louie and stalked back to the boy. "If you ever dare touch Louie again, you'll regret it for the rest of your pathetic life."

"OK, OK. Jeez, I was just joking," the boy whined, still lying on the floor.

Rose glowered at him and stomped away.

"That was fantastic," Louie exclaimed. "What a leap! What a tackle! You could be an American football star."

Rose grinned. "It *was* pretty good, wasn't it?"

Louie had survived one close call. Were more on their way? Fame was bringing dangers he never expected.

CHAPTER 16

The Tournament Starts

THE MATCHES BEGAN. Over the next two weeks, each team would play three games in the opening round. Then, the top two teams in each group of four advanced to the next round. Louie sat at the end of the French team's bench on top of an equipment box. Rose, because she was the assistant coach's daughter, was allowed to sit on the bench also.

France did well in the opening game. They defeated Japan handily, 2-0.

The stadium rocked with the chant of "*Allez les Bleus*!"—"Go Blues!" Louie got a little hoarse from yelling instructions and cheering.

Paraguay was a harder challenge, as the team had a rough, physical style of play. France managed a one to one tie. Unfortunately though, France's right defender, Christopher Mandanda, injured his leg in a tangle with a Paraguayan midfielder, and it looked like he'd be out for the rest of the tournament.

"I am so sorry," Louie consoled the dejected player. "You played really well."

For Louie, France's 3-0 victory over the United States in the first round was especially satisfying. He knew it was somewhat irrational, but he blamed the US as a whole for the invention of Mickey Mouse. Mickey Mouse was a character Louie found offensive and insulting to mice everywhere (even though he couldn't help chuckling at the antics of Mickey's friend, Donald Duck).

"Did you ever see a mouse who wears white gloves all the time?" he complained to Rouzon one night as they dined together in a bistro near the Eiffel Tower. Louie sat on a cup turned upside down on top of the table. "Plus he has a dog for a pet. It's ridiculous!"

Rouzon chuckled but he good-naturedly agreed. "*Oui, oui*, yes, yes. Of course. Completely ridiculous," he said, smiling.

After the victory over the Americans, Levi told Louie he had provided good suggestions about the placement of players and pacing of the game during the early matches. While they were relieved that France had emerged from the opening round, they all knew that now the harder games would begin. Now, all it would take would be one loss to get eliminated from the tournament. And they were worried to have lost their right defender.

France's opponent in the next round was Mexico. Louie had studied films of the Mexican games and had noticed that their left defender, Martinez, sometimes hesitated a moment when a forward was bearing down on him. He thought Michel could take advantage of this tentativeness. He discussed this observation with Casparre and Levi, and they agreed with him.

"Wait for your opportunity," Louie told Michel, "and when you sense Martinez holding back, then attack!"

The French striker followed this advice perfectly. He was patient, and in the final ten minutes with the score tied 2-2, Michel seized his opportunity. He raced past the defender and scored the winning goal.

Louie high-fived Levi and Levi low-fived Louie back.

"Yes!" Rose cheered, raising her fist into the air.

"*Allez les Bleus*!" screamed the crowd.

After the game Michel told the team, "Coach LaSurie was the one who made this win possible. I dedicate this game to him."

Inwardly, Louie was delighted, but outwardly he was modest. "If not for Michel's brilliance, even the best advice would have been for nothing. Plus, this is merely the beginning."

In the quarterfinal against Ghana five days later, France was again victorious. The team's, and indeed the whole country's, hopes were high.

Louie was in such demand for interviews with writers and broadcasters from around the world that he finally had to stop giving interviews and concentrate fully on the game to come.

Concentrating was difficult to do when he was at home at the Levis'. With all the publicity, word had leaked out where the mouse was living. Every morning, a crowd of paparazzi gathered in front of the Levis' apartment. They carried cameras, hoping for a glimpse of the diminutive celebrity.

They were a rude bunch, jostling and talking loudly throughout the day and into the night. Sometimes people even climbed on ladders to look through the windows.

Louie had to be smuggled out of the apartment each morning in Rose's pocket. He hated it in there. It was itchy and cramped. Plus it felt undignified for a member of the French coaching staff to have to sneak out, covered with lint, inside a pocket.

The gawkers pushed close to her, saying, "*Mademoiselle, mademoiselle*! What is he really like?"

"Is it true the mouse sleeps in a bowl of milk every night?"

"I heard he plays Beethoven on the tuba. Is that correct?"

"Isn't he from another planet?"

As he listened to these ridiculous questions from inside Rose's pocket, Louie couldn't help laughing. He put his paw over his mouth so no one would hear him.

To all these inquirers, Rose responded, "None of your business!" To some of the really rude people she said, "I have a good idea. Why don't you go home and get a life of your own?"

Louie thought that was an excellent suggestion.

He apologized to the Levis at supper one night. "I'm sorry I've brought such disturbance to your peaceful home."

"Don't be absurd, Louie," Madame Levi said graciously. "It's not your fault. This is the price of success."

"In any case," Coach Levi added, "it will soon pass."

Every day Louie received a letter or postcard from his mother, saying how proud of him everyone was back home, and filling him in on news of his brothers and sisters, cousins, aunts and uncles.

Louie was concerned, though, that he hadn't received any letters back from François. "I wonder if I've offended him somehow?" he thought. "I better write and check in with him." But he was preoccupied with soccer work and avoiding the paparazzi and he never found the time.

France was so successful in its run up to the semifinals that some journalists jokingly suggested that all teams hire a mouse to serve on their coaching staffs.

England, France's opponent in the semifinal, did not hire a mouse, but to Louie's chagrin they did do something almost as unusual. They hired a cat.

CHAPTER 17

An English Cat

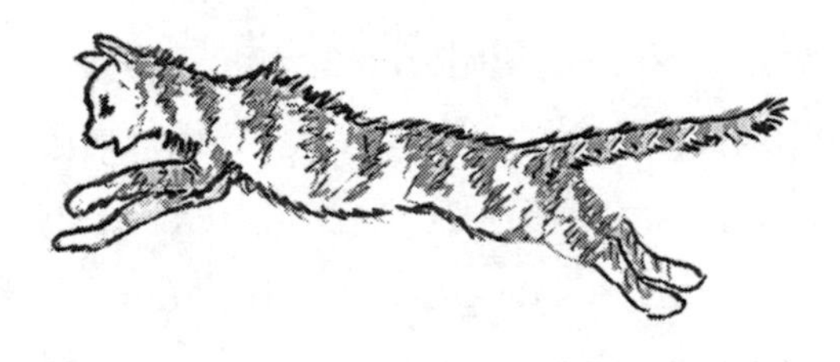

LOUIE PRAYED FOR SUCCESS as he entered the stadium for the semi-final. If France won today, they'd be in the final. If they lost, the tournament would be over for them.

At the start of the game Louie got a jolt when he noticed a large, mean-looking, orange tomcat staring rudely at him from the end of the English team's bench. "What's the mattuh, gov'nuh," the cat yelled over to Louie in a Cockney accent, "cat got yer tongue?"

The English players guffawed at Louie's obvious discomfort. They were clearly trying to unnerve and distract Louie and, through him, the French team. The two teams' benches were separated by only twenty feet of grass.

Louie gulped, but tried not to show that he was frightened. He yelled back at the cat in English. "Well, well. So England now has a cat on its team. Or is it a rat? Yes, I do think it's a rat. Or maybe it's just an ugly skunk. It's hard to tell."

"Why you!" The cat lunged toward Louie, but an English player caught it by its collar.

"I'll get you later," the cat hissed at Louie.

"Not with me here, you won't," Rose growled at the cat.

If England was trying to distract the French team with the cat, all it did was fire up the French players even more. It seemed to Louie that out of loyalty to him, the French squad played with even more intensity.

At one point in the second half, an English player tossed a water bottle toward his team's bench.

Louie laughed as the top popped off and water drenched the cat.

Shocked—the cat had been staring at Louie and not watching the game—it bolted onto the pitch, tripping one of the French players.

The referee stopped the game and gave a red card to the cat for disrupting play. With a red card, the cat had to leave the field.

"*Ciao*, Skunk Face," Louie called to the feline as it was carried away.

The cat spit at him and scratched the man who held it as it tried to escape and attack Louie.

Louie sat back in relief. Despite his brave words to the cat, and Rose's vow to defend him, he had been nervous the whole game, knowing those hungry yellow eyes were watching his every move.

Regulation time ended in a draw, and there was no further scoring in overtime. The victor would be decided in a penalty kick shootout.

Louie spoke quietly to the players who had been selected to take the first five shots for France. Their faces looked tense. "Don't overthink things," Louie told them. "Your animal nature knows exactly how to kick the ball. Relax, and your body will do the rest."

The players nodded and trotted out to the middle of the field to await their turns to kick.

If the presence of the cat had been nerve-wracking for Louie, the shootout was even worse. Despite his brave words to the players, Louie paced up and down the sideline as each team took its shots. He could hardly bear to watch.

Finally, a British player missed. It was up to Gerard. He kicked the ball confidently and scored! France had won!

Rose picked up Louie and kissed him right on the nose. They were going to the final!

CHAPTER 18

Reunion

FRANCE'S OPPONENT WOULD BE ITALY, who had defeated Brazil 2-1 in the other semifinal. All the experts on TV and in the newspapers said that Italy was way better. The experts agreed that France had very little hope of defeating the strong Italian team.

Louie did not have much respect for experts. After all, none of them had expected France to make it this far. And they all doubted his abilities as a mouse. Louie hoped desperately that he and the team could prove these so-called experts wrong once again.

When Louie walked into the coaches' office before the next practice, Coach Casparre's eyes were twitching and his fingers drumming on his thigh. Louie knew this meant he was nervous.

"Italy," Casparre spat. "They always give us trouble. *Zut.*"

"We'll just have to do the best we can," said Louie.

"Of course we will, you tiny idiot," snapped Casparre.

Louie scowled at being called a "tiny idiot." On the other hand, he was cheered that Casparre respected him enough to insult him like he insulted everyone else.

Louie managed to get tickets for the final game for his mother, father, brothers and sisters and François. Officially, the match was sold out and the stadium full, but Louie was able to persuade the stadium officials that seven mice would not take up very much space. (Stuart and Bianca, who were the oldest of Louie's siblings, had jobs and had to stay home.) With Levi's help in the matter, seven small chairs were to be set up in front of the first row near the midfield line. It was also arranged that Rose's mother would sit near the mice and be their chaperone.

The day before the final, Louie, Rose and Madame Levi met Louie's parents and siblings and François at the train station.

"Louie!" his mom screamed when she saw him. "*Mon petit Loulou*!" She ran to him and almost knocked him down, so eager was she to hug him.

Louie was mortified by his mother's gushing and squirmed within her tight embrace. He glanced at Rose to see if she had noticed his mom's nickname. Louie thought he saw her biting her lip trying not to laugh.

Louie's father slapped Louie so hard on his back that Louie did in fact go sprawling. "Sorry, *mon fils*," Monsieur LaSurie said, hoisting Louie back up to his feet.

Louie hugged Elizabeth, Martin, Bernard, and Norman.

Louie turned to François. "Hey François!" he cried. He started to run toward his friend.

"Hello," François replied coolly, taking a step back.

Louie stopped short. He gave François a puzzled look.

Before he could figure out what was going on, it was time for introductions. Paws and hands were shaken, "I've heard so much about you's" were spoken, and photos were taken.

Louie noticed that François avoided shaking hands with Rose. Louie felt a hollow sensation in his belly. Something was wrong.

As the entourage headed toward the station exit, Louie fell in beside François. "How come you never wrote back to me? What's going on?" Louie asked.

"Nothing." François sped up his steps and moved away from Louie.

"François's acting really strangely," Louie said to Rose.

Rose sighed. "Don't you get it, Louie? He's jealous."

"Jealous? Of my success?"

"No, silly. Of me."

"Oh." Louie's heart ached as he began to understand what his friend had been feeling. He caught back up with François. "François, if not for you, I'd never be here. You're my best friend and nothing will ever change that."

"Not even a stupid girl?" François snorted.

"Rose is not stupid," Louie said. "She's great. She's my friend, too. Look, François, I'm sorry you weren't able to come with me to Paris. I wish you had been able to. That would have been wonderful. But I'm happy you're here now. I'm happy you're my best friend."

François didn't say anything, but Louie thought he saw his friend's tight jaw relax a bit.

Rose and Madame Levi gave the mice a tour of Paris. François cheered up even more when they stopped at the Poilâne bakery for its famous butter cookies. By the time they arrived back at the Levis' place, François and Rose were chatting and smiling.

Louie watched them, relieved.

About half the team was going to the Shooting Star Restaurant that night for a pregame meal. The Shooting Star was known for its international menu. It featured dishes from Europe, Africa, Asia and the Americas. The players invited Louie and his guests to join them. Louie thought this would be a good opportunity for his parents and siblings and François to meet the team.

François agreed. He wanted to see the players up close, and also he loved the taste of the small paper fortunes in Chinese fortune cookies. The Shooting Star was famous for serving fortune cookies with dessert.

Coach Levi, however, had frowned when he heard that ten team members were planning to dine out that evening. "I don't get a good feeling about it. I wish they would simply lay low tonight. But they're grown men, and I'm not their father."

Because of Levi, the mice didn't go out with the team. Instead, they had a jolly dinner at home with the Levis' in their small kitchen.

Monsieur LaSurie wound up imbibing a little too much wine. He amused his hosts with some traditional mouse drinking songs, such as "Minerva the Marvelous Mouse" and "The Mice of the Round Table."

Louie sighed and rolled his eyes the whole time. His parents were so incredibly embarrassing.

But the Levis laughed heartily and asked for more.

Despite his embarrassment, Louie found that the presence of his family distracted him and eased his nervousness about the next day's final match.

Rose had prepared sleeping quarters in her closet for the guests.

Louie and François whispered together for a while as they lay in their beds. "Remember that time we took out Manoche's shoelaces, and his shoes fell off during recess?"

"Yeah, or the time you kicked your pea right through the school window?"

"I was grounded for two weeks after that."

The two friends laughed as they recalled their adventures.

For the first time in weeks, Louie fell asleep with the comforting smell of other mice nearby.

He woke early the next morning. He remembered, with a start, that today was the day of the World Cup Final. His stomach knotted up. He had to go outside, get some fresh air, clear his head.

In the half-light of dawn, Louie could see that everyone else was still sound asleep. He tiptoed out of the closet and down the hall. He climbed up onto the windowsill and peeked out the window. The paparazzi were nowhere in sight. Even they were still sleeping.

Louie pulled on his jacket, squeezed under the open window, and shimmied down a drainpipe to the ground. He began strolling down the block. It felt good to be by himself. He realized that he had been with other people almost constantly since he had arrived in Paris.

What a whirlwind it had been. So many new humans.

So many new faces. So much to learn and absorb. And how many weeks had it been since he left Marseille? Louie did some mental calculations. Only five and a half.

The eastern sky was pink and becoming brighter by the second. A mild breeze stirred his whiskers. It looked to be a fair day for the final. Ah, the final. Italy was going to be a tough and worthy opponent. Louie, Levi and Casparre had watched and analyzed films of all Italy's previous World Cup games. Louie could not detect any weaknesses on the experienced squad.

They must be vulnerable somewhere, Louie thought as he walked down the deserted, early-morning streets. As he pondered the Italian team, mentally reviewing each of their players, he was startled to hear someone speaking directly behind him.

"'ello, 'ello, 'ello. What 'ave we 'ere?" said a familiar voice in English, speaking with a Cockney accent.

Louie wheeled around. There was the cat from the match against England!

CHAPTER 19

Squiggles

THE FUR ON LOUIE'S BACK STOOD UP STRAIGHT.

"'Skunk Face,' that's what you called me," the cat sneered. "That wasn't very nice now, was it? Well, mousie, you won't be callin' me or anyone else any smart names ever ag'in. In fact, you won't be doin' anythin' ever ag'in."

The cat advanced slowly toward him, its tail swishing back and forth.

Louie glanced around. There was no help anywhere in sight. "Look," he said, backing up, "that was just in the heat of the moment. Caught up in the game and so forth."

"Right," the cat said, a vicious gleam in its eye. "No one insults Squiggles and gets away with it. Squiggles's been trackin' you ever since. Waiting for 'is moment, Squiggles 'as. 'E can be very patient when 'e needs to be."

Louie thought that in another context it would be

amusing that the cat referred to itself in the third person. And also that Squiggles was a pretty stupid name. But he didn't have the luxury of being amused. He had to think fast.

"Now Squiggles," he said. "You wouldn't want this crime on your hands—uh, paws—I mean, claws. You—"

"But you see," said the cat with a smile. "No one will know."

"That dog will know," Louie said pointing behind Squiggles. "Look out!"

The cat pivoted around, and Louie sprinted down the sidewalk. Louie heard Squiggles yell, "You louse of a mouse!" and start to give chase.

Louie darted back and forth. The cat was gaining on him. He spied a flower shop on his left. If he could only squeeze under the front door. It looked like a big enough gap for him to get under. Barely.

Louie felt the cat's hot breath on his back. He dove to get under the door. Ouch! His head bonked against the wooden frame. He scrambled frantically, trying to squirm his way under. It was no good. The gap was too small. He was trapped!

Squiggles pounced and landed with a paw on Louie's tail.

Louie stopped struggling. He turned to face his attacker. The whole world became deathly still.

"This is it, mousie." The cat chuckled. "Too bad you won't get to see the final. You'll never know 'oo won.

Ain't that a shame? The only final you'll see is your final breath."

The thought of not knowing how the game turned out gave Louie a terrible pang. Images of his parents and François and Rose and Levi and Rouzon and his other teammates flashed through his mind. It couldn't end like this.

Squiggles batted Louie with his paw. Louie's head jerked sideways, his tail still pinned by the cat's other paw. Squiggles was enjoying toying with him.

Just like a cat, Louie thought. It made him mad. "Are you going to kill me or not, Skunk Face? Come on, I don't have all day." Louie knew it was a dumb thing to say, but better to go out with style and spirit.

"You asked for it, wise guy," spat out Squiggles. He reared back his head for the death blow. Louie could see his sharp, horrible fangs.

Squiggles opened his mouth even wider and lunged toward Louie.

Louie kicked with all his might. He caught the cat square on the bottom of its jaw.

Squiggles gave a yelp of pain, and Louie slipped from his grasp. Louie's soccer skills, or at least his powerful kick, had saved his life. He darted away. Could he outrun the cat this time?

No. Squiggles cornered him once again. He slowly approached Louie, blocking off the mouse's escape path.

“Stop, you villain!” yelled a small voice.

The cat froze.

It was François, bicycling for all he was worth down the sidewalk toward them.

Squiggles laughed. “A mouse on a bike. This is too much.” His grin vanished as around the corner after François came Rose.

She was bicycling full speed, with a very determined and wild look on her face.

“Yahhh!” screamed Rose like a Mongol warrior, as she rode her bicycle right at the cat.

Squiggles bolted. He sprinted down the sidewalk with Rose right behind him. The cat darted across the street and down an alleyway.

Rose chased him until they were both out of sight.

A few minutes later, a panting Rose returned to Louie. He was sitting against the door. François sat next to him, patting his knee. François gave Louie a drink from a mouse-size water bottle.

The water tasted so good. He was still alive! "Thanks," was all he could think of to say.

"The cat climbed over a wall and got away," Rose reported. "He sure was scared, though."

"I woke up this morning with a funny feeling that you were in trouble," François said. "When I discovered you had left the apartment, I woke up Rose and we hit the streets. I borrowed your bicycle. I hope you don't mind."

"He got the knack of riding it immediately," Rose interjected with pride.

François smiled shyly. "We rode throughout the neighborhood, calling, 'Louie? Louie LaSurie?' We ran across a couple of pigeons and asked them if they had seen a mouse walk by wearing blue pants and a French team jacket. They were not too friendly and said no. Finally we met a squirrel. She said she thought she had seen a mouse fitting that description head toward this street a few minutes ago. We turned the corner, and there you were, thank God."

"If you hadn't shown up," Louie said, "I might have become breakfast for Squiggles."

"Squiggles?" Rose asked.

Louie nodded, and all three friends burst into laughter.

"Oh my gosh," Rose said, looking at her watch. "We better get home right away."

"Here's your bike," François said. "I'll ride with Rose."

Rose said, "I think you'd better ride with me, Louie. You look a little shaky still."

Rose picked up Louie and placed him in her pocket. François climbed on the small bicycle, Rose got on hers, and the three friends raced home as fast as they could.

The day of the World Cup Final had sure gotten off to an exciting start. Louie wondered what more would happen on this fateful day.

CHAPTER 20

The Final

LEVI WAS JUST PUTTING THE PHONE down as they walked into the apartment. He was pale and he looked stunned.

"What's wrong, Papa?" asked Rose.

"Ten players. Ten players," he grumbled.

"Ten players what?"

"Ten of our players are out! They can't play!"

"What? Why?"

"They all got food poisoning from that stupid restaurant," Levi said. "I knew they shouldn't have gone there. They've been vomiting all night."

Louie felt sick himself merely hearing this news. "But can't they recover?" he said. "The game won't start for several hours yet."

"No," Levi said. "The team doctor won't allow it. He said they're too dehydrated and too exhausted."

Louie did some quick calculating in his head. "But

that leaves us with only eleven players. We won't have any subs available."

Levi nodded.

Louie and Rose looked at each other. He wondered how Casparre and the team would react to this setback.

Louie soon found out. When he entered the locker room, Casparre was all alone, pacing the floor, muttering to himself and giggling. Louie thought the coach seemed hysterical, almost crazy.

"Of all the superb restaurants in Paris, they had to eat at that place last night. Ha ha. Only eleven players. Eleven players. The World Cup Final. Tee hee hee. Italy. No substitutes. *Zut!*"

Louie quietly changed clothes, trying not to attract any attention. When Casparre had calmed down a bit and stopped pacing, the coach noticed Louie. "You ever go to the Shooting Star Restaurant, LaSurie?"

"No."

"Don't."

"Uh, OK."

The coach sat on one of the benches. He sighed. It seemed to Louie like Casparre was regaining his equilibrium. "I guess it's a miracle we made it even this far," the coach said in a sober voice. "And if we win today, with only eleven men, it'll be an even bigger miracle."

"We can do it, Coach."

"I like your spirit, LaSurie. Always have."

Louie blushed. He had thought that Casparre, though respecting his opinions and suggestions, had never really cared to have a mouse on the coaching staff.

The players began entering the locker room. No one was talking or joking like they usually did.

Louie made a point to shake each player's hand and say a few words of encouragement. "Your kicking has never looked better," he told one player.

"Your defense has been great," he told another.

"Give it everything you've got," he urged another. "Don't hold back."

Each player listened carefully and said, "Thanks, Coach." But their shoulders were slumped, and Louie thought they still seemed depressed and discouraged. Despite his confident words to the men, Louie himself was terribly nervous. From time to time, he had to reach out and hold his whiskers to keep them from twitching. He kept reminding himself to take deep breaths.

Close to game time, Casparre gave an uncharacteristically emotional speech. "Men," he began, "*and* mouse..."

Everyone smiled.

"I'm proud of all of you for pulling together following the betting scandal. In fact, working with you these past weeks has been one of the joys of my career. But you know the situation. You know we're down to only eleven players. Each of you will have to stay focused and determined throughout the entire game. Each of you will have to rise to a whole new level of play. I have faith that you can do it."

Then Levi provided some last-minute strategy suggestions. "If there's anywhere Italy is vulnerable, it's down the left flank. Focus your attacks there."

The players nodded.

"Keep your temper," Levi cautioned. "Watch out for yellow cards. Remember, we don't have any subs."

Finally Louie addressed the team. He stood on top of the water cooler. He gazed at the men who had become his friends and comrades. He felt proud of all of them and of himself. The room grew silent. "I will make my speech short," he began. "Like me."

The team chuckled.

"We don't need a fortune cookie to know the challenge before us is great," Louie said.

The players groaned.

"Seriously," Louie continued. "We all know we're in a difficult position. Some might say it's an impossible position. But I don't say it's impossible. If my experience has taught me anything, it's that anything is possible."

"Hear, hear," said Philipe in English.

"Where? Where?" joked Rouzon.

Everyone laughed.

Louie thought it was a good sign. The team's mood was loosening up.

"You all know this is the opportunity of a lifetime," Louie said. "We'll remember this day for the rest of our lives. Let's make it a good memory, a happy memory. For us. For your children. For France. For everyone who loves soccer!"

"And for mice!" Michel shouted.

"Believe in possibility," Louie exhorted. "Believe we can do this. Believe we can win!"

Then the eleven players and three coaches joined their twenty-six hands and two paws in a huddle. "*Un, deux, trois, vive la France!*" they cried.

The team lined up beneath the stands in the tunnel leading to the field. Rose joined the French team there. The Italian team lined up right next to them. Louie thought their players looked big and tough. Also, compared to France, there were a lot of them, about twice as many.

The two teams ignored each other. Each player and coach on both teams was paired with a French child. They were to walk hand-in-hand with the child down the tunnel and onto the pitch for the opening ceremonies.

Louie was surprised to see that a little mouse child had been selected to walk with him. She was tiny and very shy, scared to even look up at Louie. "Monique," she said in a small, squeaky voice when Louie asked her name.

Louie noticed that Rose, as an unofficial member of the coaching staff, had been paired with a child also, a boy about her age. Neither Rose nor the boy appeared too keen to hold the other one's hand.

Finally the officials gave them the signal to enter the stadium.

Louie took Monique's paw, telling her, "Don't worry, it'll be all right." They followed the players down the

tunnel and into the bright light.

They were greeted with the loudest ovation Louie had ever heard. "*Allez les Bleus*! *Allez les Bleus*!"

Louie knew that this short-handed team with a mouse as part of the coaching staff had caught the imagination of the entire world.

Louie gazed up at the stands packed with people.

He was filled with so much nervous energy, he felt like cheering along with them. Remembering his role, he kept quiet and marched along beside Monique. He felt her little paw trembling inside his own.

France, the underdog and also the home team, was the favorite of the crowd, although a sizable and loud contingent of Italian fans were also singing and chanting with gusto.

Louie spied his parents, siblings, François and Madame Levi. He waved to them. It warmed his heart to see them there.

Elizabeth and Norman unfurled a little homemade banner that read, *Where there's a mouse, there's a way!*

Louie gave his brother and sister a thumbs-up.

François took out a tiny *vuvuzela*, the plastic horn that achieved notoriety at the 2010 World Cup in South Africa. François gave it a toot.

Louie smiled.

The national anthem of Italy was played first. Then it was France's turn. Louie sang along, although he substituted the words of the "Mouseillaise" for those of the "Marseillaise."

The head of FIFA then made a speech about antidiscrimination that Louie liked.

The coaches and subs retreated to the sidelines.

"*Au revoir*, Monique," Louie said to the little mouse, who stared at him with huge eyes before an official ushered her away to a special viewing section along with the other children.

The players took their positions on the pitch.

The referee blew his whistle and, finally, the match was underway.

The game was a rematch for the two teams who had faced each other in the 2006 World Cup Final. France had lost that game on penalty kicks after their star, Zinedine Zidane, had been ejected in overtime for his infamous head butt. It was one of the worst moments in French sporting history, and Louie prayed that this time Fate would look more kindly on his team.

The game started slowly and cautiously, each side probing and gauging its opponent. After fifteen minutes the intensity and pace of play increased.

Louie paced the sideline as the tension grew.

Both sides played with great abandon, and only incredible goaltending by both teams' keepers preserved a zero to zero tie at halftime.

The first half, though, was marred by roughness. The referee gave five yellow cards, three to Italy and two to France, for dangerous play.

In the locker room during the halftime break, France's players grumbled at the dirty tactics of the Italians and the unfairness of the referee.

"Don't get caught up in complaining about the other team or the referee," Levi warned. "Just play your game."

"Play it cool," Louie added. "Remember to make

it fun." He hoped nobody would notice his whiskers twitching, belying his brave words.

The warnings did not work.

Early in the second half, an Italian player plowed hard into Philipe, sending him sprawling.

Outraged by this dangerous attack on their goalie, the French players began screaming and swearing at the Italians, with the Italians swearing right back. The yelling turned into pushes, and the pushes escalated into punches.

Soon a dozen players were in the mix, wrestling, punching and kicking.

Louie was incensed at the hard foul on the goalkeeper. He started to bolt onto the field to join in the mêlée.

Rose jumped off the team bench and grabbed Louie's tail, jerking him back. "What are you doing?" she hissed.

"Let me go!" Louie screamed, in full battle mode. "They can't treat Philipe like that. Let me go!"

But Rose hung on to his tail while Louie flailed and struggled to get loose and join in the rumble that was raging in the goalbox. Gradually he calmed down. "Thanks, Rose," Louie said at last, a little embarrassed. "I probably wouldn't have been much help in the fight anyway."

"You probably would've gotten yourself killed, you crazy mouse," Rose said. "That's probably what would've happened."

When all the fighting players were finally separated

and it quieted down on the field, the referee and the two assistant-referee linesmen conferred with each other. The head ref wound up holding up two red cards. One player on each side was immediately thrown out of the game. Then the ref gave yellow cards to two other players on each side. It was the second one in the game for all four of them, and this meant they were eliminated from the game also. Teams were not allowed to replace ejected players with substitutes. It was now eight versus eight on the field.

"This isn't good," Louie said to Rose. "With only eight players and no subs, our players are going to get exhausted having to cover so much territory."

About ten minutes later, Italy earned a corner kick and their tall forward, Paolo Giancarlo, timed his jump perfectly and headed the kick into the corner of the net. A brilliant goal. The Italian fans went crazy.

The French supporters stared glumly at the Italian players hugging each other and celebrating on the field.

Louie spit on the ground. "Drat and double drat!"

"Don't worry, Louie," Rose said. "There's plenty of time left."

It sounded to Louie like Rose wasn't as confident as she pretended, but it turned out she was right. France came storming back. Rouzon passed to Michel, who feinted right and then passed back to a streaking Rouzon, who eluded a defender and blasted a shot into the goal. The score was now 1-1.

Rose gave Louie a low-five. "Told you!" she said.

The game moved back and forth, both teams playing strongly and defending well. However, some of the French players were starting to falter with fatigue.

Italy substituted in two players with fresh legs. They sprinted onto the pitch as if to show off how rested and energized they were.

Louie and Rose exchanged a rueful look. Italy now seemed to have the upper hand. This was what Louie had been afraid of.

Suddenly, disaster struck. Two French defenders and one Italian vied to head a cross pass in front of the French goal, and the French players clunked heads with each other and fell to the ground.

"Oh no!" Louie cried, wringing his paws.

Philipe cleared the ball out of bounds, and the referee paused the game.

The emergency medical crew ran onto the pitch.

The crowd grew silent.

Rose grasped Louie's paw.

After a few moments, the head medic trotted back to the French bench. Both French players had suffered concussions, she reported, and were not fit to play any longer.

They were bundled onto stretchers and carried off the pitch.

France was now down to only six players. But a team needed at least seven players on the field or it would be forced to forfeit the game!

The French coaches conferred, trying to figure out what to do. The referee blew his whistle for the game to resume.

"Put me in, Coach," Louie pleaded. "I'll be the seventh man."

"Now's not the time for one of your cute jokes," Casparre snapped.

"I'm not joking. Put me in."

The ref blew his whistle again. It sounded sharper and shorter this time.

Casparre and Levi talked frantically. They couldn't think of a better plan than the one Louie had suggested.

"All right, you're in, LaSurie," Casparre finally growled. "Just stay out of the way and don't get squished."

I'm in! I'm in! Louie thought. Another thought immediately followed. *Oh no! I'm in*. He gulped. All of a sudden he felt very, very small.

CHAPTER 21

"*Allez* LaSurie!"

THE STADIUM ANNOUNCER INTONED over the loudspeaker, "Now entering the game for France, number ninety-nine, Louie LaSurie."

The crowd roared. Louie glanced at the stands and spied his father, brothers and sister and Francois shouting wildly and jumping up and down. He couldn't spot his mother. François later told him that in all the excitement, they failed to notice that Louie's mother had fainted.

A thousand cameras flashed as Louie jogged across the chalk sideline onto the pitch. He reached down with his right paw and touched the grass, and then kissed his paw for good luck. His heart was beating hard. This was it. The opportunity of a lifetime.

The Italian coach immediately protested. He ran onto the field right up to the head referee, his arms gesticulating wildly. "France can't use a mouse as a player!" he yelled.

The referee said, "I see your point."

"Excuse me, *monsieur*," Louie said to the ref, "but there's nothing in the FIFA rulebook that says a mouse can't play."

The referee stared at him.

"It's true," Louie said. "I checked."

The ref scowled at Louie. He waved Louie away, and he and the two linesmen walked to the center circle to confer.

The stadium grew silent once again as everyone awaited their decision.

Louie stood among his teammates on the edge of the pitch. He gazed all around the hushed stadium and then back to the center of the field. *Please let me play*, he prayed.

The referee and the linesmen searched through the rulebook. Like Louie said, they could find nothing that prohibited a mouse from playing on an international soccer team. The referee walked up to the Italian coach. "Sorry, *Signore*," he reported. "The mouse can play."

The Italian coach threw up his hands, and all the Italian players argued, but the referee stood firm.

Louie shouted, "Yes!" He jumped up and down, beaming at all his teammates. And then his grin suddenly vanished as the dangerous reality of the situation struck him. He blew out his breath through pursed lips. He'd have to be very alert out there on the field. Like Old Giresse had told him, he'd really have to be ready for anything now.

The referee blew his whistle. The game resumed.

The crowd cheered. Their chant changed from "*Allez Les Bleus*" to "*Allez* LaSurie."

Louie was stationed as a defender. France's strategy, being so shorthanded, was to concentrate on defense and hope for an opportunity to counterattack.

It was hard for Louie to see everything that was happening. The players near him loomed like skyscrapers. Fortunately his soccer instincts and knowledge of the game helped him stay oriented.

The French team played courageously.

Italy kept pressing. A kick came in Louie's direction just outside the penalty box.

He ran to meet the ball.

The Italian forward, Giovanni Ciminello, ran toward him.

Now that he was actually playing, Louie was no longer quite so nervous. He didn't have time to jump on top of the ball and start running, but he kicked with all his might and deflected the ball about two and a half inches.

The ball moved just enough to throw off Ciminello's timing. The Italian kicked at empty air and then stumbled and fell.

He sprawled dramatically on the ground, grimacing and moaning and clutching his shin in apparent pain. "He tripped me! He tripped me!" Ciminello yelled to the referee.

The referee blew his whistle. He awarded a free kick to Italy.

Ciminello smirked at the mouse.

Louie ran up to the referee. "I didn't trip him. He flopped!"

The referee ignored Louie, which made the mouse even angrier. He kicked the referee's shoe to get his attention. "He took a dive, I tell you!"

"Yellow card!" yelled the referee. He pulled the card from his pocket and held it over his head. He wrote Louie's name and uniform number in his notebook. Apparently, the referee didn't like his judgment being questioned by a mouse, not to mention being kicked by one.

The crowd whistled their disapproval of the ref and the Italian.

Louie was furious, his paws bunched into fists, but his teammates ushered him away from the referee before he got in any more trouble and was thrown out of the game.

"Calm down, Louie," Rouzon, the team captain, warned. "You're playing well. Just calm down. We can't afford to lose you."

Louie knew Rouzon was correct. If he lost his temper and got another yellow card, he'd be kicked out of the game and France would forfeit.

Ciminello jumped back to his feet, miraculously healed from the injury Louie had supposedly given him. He kicked the free kick hard and it curved past the wall of French defenders. It headed toward the corner of the goal. Would it go in? The ball deflected off the goalpost, and Philipe kicked the ball clear.

The Italian fans groaned and the French fans sighed in relief.

Louie wiped the sweat out of his eyes and grinned at Rouzon.

Play continued and Italy dominated but couldn't quite score. After controlling the ball for long stretches, the Italians were caught off-guard when France suddenly launched a counterattack and earned a corner kick.

Louie moved upfield for the corner kick and stood near Ciminello.

While the ref wasn't looking, Ciminello nudged Louie with his shoe, not hard enough to attract attention from others, but hard enough to hurt.

"Ow! Bug off," Louie said.

Ciminello smirked. "I saw your mother in the stands there. Wow, she's ugly! She's so ugly, mousetraps run away from *her*. And what about your sister? They say she smells so bad, you'd swear she was a rat, not a mouse."

Louie felt his temper swelling. Ciminello was like all the bullies he had ever faced rolled into one. Mean. Cheating. Arrogant. Louie felt an almost irresistible urge to head-butt the Italian. He'd hit Ciminello right in the soft inner part of the ankle. That would hurt.

Louie reared his head back to prepare for the strike.

Just then, the lines he had written for Madame Lambert popped into his mind. *I will not lose my temper.* Louie took a breath and thought, *He wants me to commit a foul and get thrown out of the game.* Louie laughed. He would not take the bait.

Ciminello was the one who was mad now. "What are you laughing at?" he snarled, but at that moment the corner kick was struck.

The Italian keeper punched it away, and Italy came storming back.

Louie retreated to his position near the French goal.

A series of beautiful Italian passes led to a shot like a rocket toward the goal. Philipe leapt and barely managed to get part of his hand on the ball. This slowed the ball down but did not stop it completely. With the French goalkeeper sprawled on the ground and the other defenders out of position, the ball was rolling slowly toward the goal line. It looked like it was bound to roll in for the winning goal for Italy.

Unseen by the crowd and even by most of the players, Louie ran toward the ball and kicked it right in the sweet spot, the way François had coached him back home in Marseille. The ball stopped rolling toward the goal and bounced an inch or two in the other direction.

Ciminello was bearing down on it, but Louie's deflection gave one of his teammates time to rush over and clear the ball off the goal line before the Italian could reach it. Louie had prevented a goal! He felt his chest swell with pride. He was actually helping the team.

The crisis was over. The score was still tied. Philipe picked up Louie and hugged him.

"You're tickling me," he complained, and the goalkeeper set Louie back down on his rear paws.

Louie looked over at the sidelines in time to see the Italian coach swear, kick at the grass, lose his balance and fall down.

Louie laughed along with the crowd.

The crowd chanted louder than ever, "*Allez* LaSurie."

Three minutes later, there was a scramble for the ball near the French goal. Louie was right in the mix of players. It was against his nature to stay out of the way like Casparre had told him.

Louie ran toward the place he thought the ball would land.

Giancarlo leapt up to head the ball. Somehow Louie wound up directly beneath the Italian. Giancarlo missed the header.

Looking up, Louie saw the bottom of Giancarlo's cleats heading straight toward him as the Italian striker returned to the earth following his leap.

Louie tried to move to the side but he slipped. Giancarlo's left foot came down right on top of him! Everything went black.

CHAPTER 22

The Most Remarkable Game in World Cup History

THE CROWD GASPED AND THEN FELL SILENT.

The referee blew his whistle, halting play. The emergency medical crew ran onto the field.

Before anyone could stop her, Rose sprinted onto the field right behind them.

"Hey, come back here!" yelled a policeman.

But Levi stopped him. "It's all right. Let her go."

Louie's teammates and Rose all gathered around the fallen mouse. The silence in the packed stadium was eerie.

The head medic took out a stethoscope and checked for Louie's pulse. She frowned. She moved the stethoscope to a different position. "Ah, there it is," she said. "Thank God." The soft grass had cushioned the force of the blow and saved Louie's life.

The medic put smelling salts under Louie's nose.

He regained consciousness, disoriented, muttering, "I'll get you, Mean Manoche." He tried to stand up, but teetered on his feet.

The medics made him stay down while they examined him, using a magnifying glass to look up close.

"He has a sprained arm," one of the medics announced, "but the rest of him seems to be fine."

The medics wanted to put his arm in a splint, but they didn't have anything small enough to use.

"I know," Rose said. "You can use part of my barrette." She removed the barrette from her hair and snapped off a piece. It was exactly the right size for Louie's arm.

"This is perfect," the medic said. She sprayed Louie's arm with a liquid. "This will feel super cold," she told Louie. "It'll stop the swelling and make your arm numb." She then placed the barrette on Louie's arm and wrapped it with a piece of tape. "How's that?"

Louie stood up gingerly. The people's faces looked blurry. He wobbled and almost fell over.

The medic put her finger on his back to steady him.

As Louie got used to standing upright once again, his vision cleared and his balance returned to normal. He jogged in place, sensing his arm and testing his legs. "It feels all right," he reported. Louie gazed around at Rose and his teammates all staring at him with grave concern. Never had they seemed so dear to him. Never had the green grass smelled so good, or the breeze felt so deliciously pleasant.

"Are you sure you feel up to staying in the game?" the medic asked.

"*Oui. Bien sûr.*" Louie looked over to where his family and Francois were sitting and gave them a thumbs-up.

Seeing him back on his feet, the crowd roared, "*Allez* LaSurie. *Allez* LaSurie."

Rose and the medical crew trotted off the field.

The game started again. The score was still one to one.

Louie's arm was numb from the cold spray, but his legs were fine, and his head was clear. His nervousness was now completely gone. The accident had wiped that away. All that was left was gratitude for being alive and a fierce desire to play.

Italy kept pressing, and France defended well. With only about a minute to play in regulation time, a ball was hit hard in Louie's direction. Just like he had practiced so many times with Rose, Louie hopped onto the ball and began running on top of it, propelling it forward swiftly with his nimble feet.

This maneuver caught the Italian and French players alike by surprise.

Louie dribbled past three dazed Italians. He was moving amazingly fast, faster than ever before. The rotating ball felt good under his feet. He saw the spots on the ball merging into a blur as he picked up speed.

Amid all the crowd noise, he thought he heard Rose's voice cheering, "Go, Louie!"

He dribbled the ball up the left side of the field, outrunning two tired Italians. Louie had fresh legs, and most of his opponents were drained from playing shorthanded and having to cover a lot of area on the pitch. Finally he rode the ball right up to the feet of his teammate, Michel, who had run to meet him.

"Jump off, Louie, jump off!" Michel yelled. Louie leapt off the ball an instant before Michel kicked it forward toward Rouzon who was streaking toward the goal. Louie rolled onto his good side, keeping the injured arm off the ground.

Rouzon blasted the ball on his first touch. Louie saw the ball go flying hard toward the corner of the net. It looked like it was certain to go in, but the Italian goalie stretched his long body and deflected the ball mere inches past the upright.

France had almost scored thanks to Louie. The crowd groaned and then cheered.

The stadium announcer said, "This is the most remarkable game in World Cup history."

Although France had missed getting a goal, at least they had earned a corner kick. Most of the French team, including Louie, moved forward into the Italian penalty area.

This is where we score, Louie thought.

But he was wrong. The goalie leapt above the crowd of players around him and punched away the corner kick.

"*Zut*!" Louie swore. He didn't have time to be

disappointed. The Italians came swarming back up the pitch.

Louie spotted an official on the sideline holding up a sign showing that three additional minutes had been added because of injury timeouts.

Michel stole the ball from Giancarlo at midfield. Michel dribbled around two Italians and passed to Rouzon on the right.

Meanwhile, Louie, unseen by any of the Italians, sprinted down the far left side of the field. He was undefended and wide open. He waved his good arm over his head, trying to get Rouzon's attention.

Only Rose, standing on top of the French team's bench, seemed to notice the tiny mouse. "Rouzon!" she screamed, her high, clear, child's voice piercing through the din of the crowd. "Louie's open on the left!"

Rouzon glanced up and spotted Louie all alone on the other side of the pitch. He lofted a pass up and over all the other players.

Most of the crowd groaned. A few Italians laughed and cheered.

Louie thought that the spectators and the players assumed that Rouzon had kicked the ball away, in a terrible mistake, wasting the opportunity.

In fact, the pass came straight to Louie. The mouse jumped on top of the ball and started running.

The Italians realized their mistake too late. They were out of position. Louie had a straight path toward the goal, with only Ciminello and the goalie in his way.

Louie dribbled fast in a complete circle to avoid Ciminello's outstretched foot.

The Italian, twisting himself to keep up with the surprising movements of the mouse, got his two feet tangled with each other and fell down.

There was no foul and the ref did not blow the whistle. "Play on," he ordered.

Louie was now only twelve feet from the goal. Out of the corner of his eye he saw two more Italians running desperately toward him.

The goalie charged toward the mouse. His red goalie gloves looked enormous to Louie, like the huge hands of a giant.

Louie faked left. He faked right. He faked left again. He thought that the starts and stops of the ball, without the body clues of a human player to indicate the possible direction of the ball, might confuse the keeper. Louie was right. The goalie lunged toward Louie clumsily.

Now! Louie thought, and he sped past the enormous hands of the goalie. He rode the ball right between the bewildered keeper's legs. Louie didn't even realize he had scored until he heard the roar of the crowd.

"Goaaalll!" Rose screamed, jumping up and down on the team bench.

"Goaaalll!" television and radio announcers from all over the world yelled into their microphones.

"Goaaalll!" shouted François, throwing his *vuvuzela* up into the air.

"Goaaalll!" rejoiced Louie's parents, hugging each other.

"Goaaalll!" cried the baker back in Marseille.

"Goaaalll!" yelled Stuart and Bianca from under the baker's couch.

"Goaaalll!" hollered Laurent and Pascal, the two tough mice in the Paris train station.

"Goaaalll!" cheered Gaston, the library janitor.

"Goaalll!" chuckled Old Giresse from behind his garbage can.

"Goaaalll!" exulted the fans in the stadium.

The referee looked at his watch and gave two tweets on his whistle. The game was over. France had won!

CHAPTER 23

World Cup Mouse

LOUIE LAY ON HIS BACK IN THE GOAL AREA, dazed and panting from his epic run on top of the ball.

The stadium crowd chanted, "Lou-ie! Lou-ie! Lou-ie!"

Louie spotted his teammates sprinting toward him. For a moment, he feared that in their euphoria they would forget he was a mouse and jump on top of him in a happy heap, crushing him. But instead Rouzon lifted the mouse onto his shoulder.

Coach Levi and Coach Casparre and Rose ran onto the field to congratulate the team. Casparre shook Louie's paw and Levi kissed him on each cheek.

Louie and Rose just looked into each other's eyes, beaming. Louie couldn't remember ever being so happy or so in love with life.

Then it was time for the head of FIFA to award the World Cup trophy to France. Rouzon hoisted it over his head and the crowd roared.

Philipe picked up Louie from Rouzon's shoulder and placed him on the golden orb of the earth that formed the top of the trophy. It was a little slippery, but Louie gripped tight with his back paws and one good front paw and was able to hold on. The World Cup felt pleasantly cool against his sweaty fur.

The team jogged a victory lap around the field with Rouzon holding the cup, and Louie riding it. Louie and the rest of the team waved to the fans. It seemed like a dream to the mouse, the most wonderful dream.

As they passed the Italian team's bench, Louie was surprised to see some of the Italian players clapping. He locked eyes with Ciminello, the player who had fouled him and insulted Louie's mother and sister.

The Italian smiled and shrugged as if to say, "Nothing personal. It was only part of the game."

Louie tried to scowl at Ciminello, but he was so happy right now and the Italian's expression was so funny that Louie couldn't help smiling back.

Then he spied his family and Francois. They were all cheering and jumping up and down.

François yelled, "*Allez* LaSurie!" He gave a triumphant blast on his little *vuvuzela*.

Louie's father shouted, "Where there's a mouse, there's a way!"

Louie's heart soared with pride and love for his family and François.

The French team continued circling the field, Louie's teammates shouting and singing and dancing as they held the cup aloft with Louie still perched on top, holding on with three paws and waving to everybody with his splint-stabilized paw.

He had done it. His dream had come true. Not only was he the first mouse to play in a World Cup tournament, he was the first mouse to ride on the actual cup itself.

He truly had become a World Cup mouse.

La Fin

Thank you for reading *World Cup Mouse*. Louie and I hope you enjoyed the book!

Do you have a question or a message for me or Louie? If so, please go to www.richardseidman.com, and let us know what it is. You can also sign up there to subscribe to my blog and writing updates.

Be in touch with Louie on Facebook at: www.facebook.com/RichardLSeidman

Reviews help other readers find books. I appreciate your reviews and comments on Goodreads, Library Thing, Amazon, Barnes and Noble, etc.

Support your local independent bookstore! And please support organizations that support youth soccer, such as the American Youth Soccer Association, Soccer Without Borders, and Play Soccer International.

Allez LaSurie!

Richard Seidman
Ashland, Oregon USA
May 2014

Acknowledgments

Thank you to the many members of Louie LaSurie's team who made it possible for this book to take the field:

To Dov, Elisha and Beth Hirschfield; Manoj Bhukar, Chandani Shrestha and Inge Hindel; Mason, Leo and Angela Decker; Ruth Resch; Julia Vaughns; Debbie Zaslow; and John and Patricia Ciminello for your friendship, enthusiasm, suggestions, and encouragement.

To Chris Eboch, Nancy Coffelt, and Angelle Pilkington for your incisive critiques and edits.

To Johanna Mitchell for your sage advice to pursue my writing wholeheartedly.

To Stephen Victor for your affirmation of my writing path.

To Paul Richards for your energetic support and coaching.

To Martín Prechtel for your profound teachings and your example of diligence in art and serving the Holy in Nature.

To Todd Wilson for sharing your expertise so generously in creating the video for the Kickstarter campaign and the World Cup Mouse book trailer.

To all the Kickstarter patrons who contributed $100 or more to help this book come to life, namely:

Andrea Bell, Bethany King, Brandy Carson, Chris Robertson, Darlene Larson, Dick and Linda Craig, Donnie and Jennifer Yance, Earth and Spirit Council, Gary Shell, Ilan Shamir, James Meisner, Janene McNeil, Jennifer Maslow, John Marrett, Kathryn Thomas, Kymberli Colbourne, Margaret Rosenau and Chris Brainard, Marilyn Zimmerwoman and Roxy Lenzo, Rachael R. Resch, Randee Fox, Paula Boggs and Jada Boggs, Rich Dinkin and Shelley Ring, Roque Neto, Ruth Resch, Toni Lavaglia.

To all the other Kickstarter supporters.

To the talented and dedicated members of my children's book writing critique group: Barbara Head, Robin Heald, Shawna Kastin, Diane Nichols and Sara-Lynne Simpson, for your skillful editorial suggestions, advice, and encouragement.

To Doris Brook, Isabel Alzado, Noel Chatroux, and Susanne Petermann for your help with French phrases and idioms.

To SCBWI and SCBWI Oregon for all the resources and support you provide.

To Stephen Mooser and Lin Oliver of SCBWI for your helpful suggestions.

To Lara Perkins and Mallory Kass for your input and suggestions at Andrea Brown Literary Agency's Big Sur Writing Workshop.

To Chris Molé for your elegant book design.

To Ursula Andrejczuk for your gorgeous illustrations that so beautifully capture the spirit of Louie and the story.

To Jill Bailin and Gillian Smith for your proofreading.

To Julie Schoerke, Marissa DeCuir Curnutte, Samantha Lien and the rest of the JKS Communications team for your great work spreading the word about *World Cup Mouse*.

To David Doersch for your brilliant narration of the World Cup Mouse audio book.

To anyone else who contributed to the creation of this book whom I've forgotten to mention here. Please forgive me.

To my parents of blessed memory, Phoebe and Herbert Seidman, for your financial support, encouragement, and love.

To my beloved wife, Rachael Resch, the center of my universe, for everything!

To you, the reader, for immersing yourself in the world of Louie LaSurie.

And to the Spirit of Play. May it permeate our lives and help make Life live.

About the Author

RICHARD SEIDMAN lives in Ashland, Oregon, USA with his wife and chickens and many stuffed animals and other small friends. You can find out more about Richard and his books at:

Website:
www.richardseidman.com
Facebook at:
www.facebook.com/RichardLSeidman
Twitter:
http://twitter.com/RLSeidman

CPSIA information can be obtained at www.ICGtesting.com
Printed in the USA
BVOW03s0356010515

398192BV00008B/227/P